The Daughter Of The Storage

By
William Dean Howells

The Daughter of the Storage

I

They were getting some of their things out to send into the country, and Forsyth had left his work to help his wife look them over and decide which to take and which to leave. The things were mostly trunks that they had stored the fall before; there were some tables and Colonial bureaus inherited from his mother, and some mirrors and decorative odds and ends, which they would not want in the furnished house they had taken for the summer. There were some canvases which Forsyth said he would paint out and use for other subjects, but which, when he came to look at again, he found really not so bad. The rest, literally, was nothing but trunks; there were, of course, two or three boxes of books. When they had been packed closely into the five-dollar room, with the tables and bureaus and mirrors and canvases and decorative odds and ends put carefully on top, the Forsyths thought the effect very neat, and laughed at themselves for being proud of it.

They spent the winter in Paris planning for the summer in America, and now it had come May, a month which in New York is at its best, and in the Constitutional Storage Safe-Deposit Warehouse is by no means at its worst. The Constitutional Storage is no longer new, but when the Forsyths were among the first to store there it was up to the latest moment in the modern perfections of a safe-deposit warehouse. It was strictly fire-proof; and its long, white, brick-walled, iron-doored corridors, with their clean concrete floors, branching from a central avenue to the tall windows north and south, offered perspectives sculpturesquely bare, or picturesquely heaped with arriving or departing household stuff.

When the Forsyths went to look at it a nice young fellow from the office had gone with them; running ahead and switching on rows of electrics down the corridors, and then, with a wire-basketed electric lamp, which he twirled about and held aloft and alow, showing the dustless, sweet-smelling spaciousness of a perfect five-dollar room. He said it would more than hold their things; and it really held them.

Now, when the same young fellow unlocked the iron door and set it wide, he said he would get them a man, and he got Mrs. Forsyth a gilt armchair from some furniture going into an adjoining twenty-dollar room. She sat down in it, and "Of course," she said, "the pieces I want will be at the very back and the very bottom. Why don't you get yourself a chair, too, Ambrose? What are you looking at?"

With his eyes on the neighboring furniture he answered, "Seems to be the wreck of a millionaire's happy home; parlor and kitchen utensils and office furniture all in white and gold."

"Horrors, yes!" Mrs. Forsyth said, without turning her head from studying her trunks, as if she might divine their contents from their outside.

"Tata and I," her husband said, "are more interested in the millionaire's things." Tata, it appeared, was not a dog, but a child; the name was not the diminutive of her own name, which was Charlotte, but a generic name for a doll, which Tata had learned from her Italian nurse to apply to all little girls and had got applied to herself by her father. She was now at a distance down the corridor, playing a drama with the pieces of millionaire furniture; as they stretched away in variety and splendor they naturally suggested personages of princely quality, and being touched with her little forefinger tip were capable of entering warmly into Tata's plans for them.

Her mother looked over her shoulder toward the child. "Come here, Tata," she called, and when Tata, having enjoined some tall mirrors to secrecy with a frown and a shake of the head, ran to her, Mrs. Forsyth had forgotten why she had called her. "Oh!" she said, recollecting, "do you know which your trunk is, Tata? Can you show mamma? Can you put your hand on it?"

The child promptly put her hand on the end of a small box just within her tiptoe reach, and her mother said, "I do believe she knows everything that's in it, Ambrose! That trunk has got to be opened the very first one!"

The man that the young fellow said he would send showed at the far end of the corridor, smaller than human, but enlarging himself to the average Irish bulk as he drew near. He was given instructions and obeyed with caressing irony Mrs. Forsyth's order to pull out Tata's trunk first, and she found the key in a large tangle of keys, and opened it, and had the joy of seeing everything recognized by the owner: doll by doll, cook-stove, tin dishes, small brooms, wooden animals on feet and wheels, birds of various plumage, a toy piano, a dust-pan, alphabet blocks, dog's-eared linen Mother Goose books, and the rest. Tata had been allowed to put the things away herself, and she took them out with no apparent sense of the time passed since she saw them last. In the changing life of her parents all times and places were alike to her. She began to play with the things in the storage corridor as if it were yesterday when she saw them last in the flat. Her mother and father left her to them in the distraction of their own trunks. Mrs. Forsyth had these spread over the space toward the window and their lids lifted and tried to decide about them. In the end she had changed the things in them back and forth till she candidly owned that she no longer knew where anything at all was.

As she raised herself for a moment's respite from the problem she saw at the far end of the corridor a lady with two men, who increased in size like her own man as they approached. The lady herself seemed to decrease, though she remained of a magnificence to match the furniture, and looked like it as to her dress of white picked out in gold when she arrived at the twenty-dollar room next the Forsyths'. In her advance she had been vividly played round by a little boy, who ran forward and back and easily doubled the length of the corridor before he came to a stand and remained with his brown eyes fixed on Tata. Tata herself had blue eyes, which now hovered dreamily above the things in her trunk.

The two mothers began politely to ignore each other. She of the twenty-dollar room directed the men who had come with her, and in a voice of authority and appeal at once commanded and consulted them in the disposition of her belongings. At the sound of the mixed tones Mrs. Forsyth signaled to her husband, and, when he came within whispering, murmured: "Pittsburg, or Chicago. Did you ever hear such a Mid-Western accent!" She pretended to be asking him about repacking the trunk before her, but the other woman was not deceived. She was at least aware of criticism in the air of her neighbors, and she put on greater severity with the workmen. The boy came up and caught her skirt. "What?" she said, bending over. "No, certainly not. I haven't time to attend to you. Go off and play. Don't I tell you no? Well, there, then! Will you get that trunk out where I can open it? That small one there," she said to one of the men, while the other rested for both. She stooped to unlock the trunk and flung up the lid. "Now if you bother me any more I will surely—" But she lost herself short of the threat and began again to seek counsel and issue orders.

The boy fell upon the things in the trunk, which were the things of a boy, as those in Tata's trunk were the things of a girl, and to run with them, one after another, to Tata and to pile them in gift on the floor beside her trunk. He did not stop running back and forth as fast as his short, fat legs could carry him till he had reached the bottom of his box, chattering constantly and taking no note of the effect with Tata. Then, as she made no response whatever to his munificence, he began to be abashed and to look pathetically from her to her father.

"Oh, really, young man," Forsyth said, "we can't let you impoverish yourself at this rate. What have you said to your benefactor, Tata? What are you going to give him?"

The children did not understand his large words, but they knew he was affectionately mocking them.

"Ambrose," Mrs. Forsyth said, "you mustn't let him."

"I'm trying to think how to hinder him, but it's rather late," Forsyth answered, and then the boy's mother joined in.

"Indeed, indeed, if you can, it's more than I can. You're just worrying the little girl," she said to the boy.

"Oh no, he isn't, dear little soul," Mrs. Forsyth said, leaving her chair and going up to the two children. She took the boy's hand in hers. "What a kind boy! But you know my little girl mustn't take all your playthings. If you'll give her one she'll give you one, and that will be enough. You can both play with them all for the present." She referred her suggestion to the boy's mother, and the two ladies met at the invisible line dividing the five-dollar room from the twenty-dollar room.

"Oh yes, indeed," the Mid-Westerner said, willing to meet the New-Yorker half-way. "You're taking things out, I see. I hardly know which is the worst: taking out or putting in."

"Well, we are just completing the experience," Mrs. Forsyth said. "I shall be able to say better how I feel in half an hour."

"You don't mean this is the first time you've stored? I suppose we've been in and out of storage twenty times. Not in this warehouse exactly; we've never been here before."

"It seems very nice," Mrs. Forsyth suggested.

"They all do at the beginning. I suppose if we ever came to the end they would seem nicer still. Mr. Bream's business is always taking him away" (it appeared almost instantly that he was the international inspector of a great insurance company's agencies in Europe and South America), "and when I don't go with him it seems easier to break up and go into a hotel than to go on housekeeping. I don't know that it is, though," she questioned. "It's so hard to know what to do with the child in a hotel."

"Yes, but he seems the sort that you could manage with anywhere," Mrs. Forsyth agreed and disagreed.

His mother looked at him where he stood beaming upon Tata and again joyfully awaiting some effect with her. But the child sat back upon her small heels with her eyes fixed on the things in her trunk and made no sign of having seen the heaps of his gifts.

The Forsyths had said to each other before this that their little girl was a queer child, and now they were not so much ashamed of her apparent selfishness or rude indifference as they thought they were. They made a joke of it with the boy's mother, who said she did not believe Tata was anything but shy. She said she often told Mr. Bream that she did wish Peter—yes, that was his name; she didn't like it much, but it was his grandfather's; was Tata a Christian name? Oh, just a pet name! Well, it was pretty—could be broken of his ridiculous habit; most children—little boys, that was—held onto their things so.

Forsyth would have taken something from Tata and given it to Peter; but his wife would not let him; and he had to content himself with giving Peter a pencil of his own that drew red at one end and blue at the other, and that at once drew a blue boy, that looked like Peter, on the pavement. He told Peter not to draw a boy now, but wait till he got home, and then be careful not to draw a blue boy with the red end. He helped him put his things back into his trunk, and Peter seemed to enjoy that, too.

Tata, without rising from her seat on her heels, watched the restitution with her dreamy eyes; she paid no attention to the blue boy on the pavement; pictures from her father were nothing new to her. The mothers parted with expressions of mutual esteem in spite of their difference of accent and fortune. Mrs. Forsyth asked if she might not kiss Peter, and did so; he ran to his mother and whispered to her; then he ran back and gave Tata so great a hug that she fell over from it.

Tata did not cry, but continued as if lost in thought which she could not break from, and that night, after she had said her prayers with her mother, her mother thought it was time to ask her: "Tata, dear, why did you act so to that boy to-day? Why didn't you give him something of yours when he brought you all his things? Why did you act so oddly?"

Tata said something in a voice so low that her mother could not make it out.

"What did you say?"

"I couldn't tell which," the child still whispered; but now her mother's ear was at her lips.

"How, which?"

"To give him. The more I looked," and the whisper became a quivering breath, "the more I couldn't tell which. And I wanted to give them all to him, but I couldn't tell whether it would be right, because you and papa gave them to me for birthday and Christmas," and the quivering breath broke into a sobbing grief, so that the mother had to catch the child up to her heart.

"Dear little tender conscience!" she said, still wiping her eyes when she told the child's father, and they fell into a sweet, serious talk about her before they slept. "And I was ashamed of her before that woman! I know she misjudged her; but we ought to have remembered how fine and precious she is, and known how she must have suffered, trying to decide."

"Yes, conscience," the father said. "And temperament, the temperament to which decision is martyrdom."

"And she will always have to be deciding! She'll have to decide for you, some day, as I do now; you are very undecided, Ambrose—she gets it from you."

II

The Forsyths were afraid that Tata might want to offer Peter some gift in reparation the next morning, and her father was quite ready, if she said so, to put off their leaving town, and go with her to the Constitutional Storage, which was the only address of Mrs. Bream that he knew. But the child had either forgotten or she was contented with her mother's comforting, and no longer felt remorse.

One does not store the least of one's personal or household gear without giving a hostage to storage, a pledge of allegiance impossible to break. No matter how few things one puts in, one never takes everything out; one puts more things in. Mrs. Forsyth went to the warehouse with Tata in the fall before they sailed for another winter in Paris, and added some old bits she had picked up at farm-houses in their country drives, and they filled the room quite to the top. She told her husband how Tata had entered into the spirit of putting back her trunk of playthings with the hope of seeing it again in the spring; and she added that she had now had to take a seven-fifty room without consulting him, or else throw away the things they had brought home.

During the ten or twelve years that followed, the Forsyths sometimes spent a whole winter in a hotel; sometimes they had a flat; sometimes they had a separate dwelling. If their housing was ample, they took almost everything out of storage; once they got down to a two-dollar bin, and it seemed as if they really were leaving the storage altogether. Then, if they went into a flat that was nearly all studio, their furniture went back in a cataclysmal wave to the warehouse, where a ten-dollar room, a twelve-dollar room, would not dam the overflow.

Tata, who had now outgrown her pet name, and was called Charlotte because her mother felt she ought to be, always went with her to the storage to help look the things over, to see the rooms emptied down to a few boxes, or replenished to bursting. In the first years she played about, close to her mother; as she grew older she ventured further, and began to make friends with other little girls who had come with their mothers. It was quite safe socially to be in the Constitutional Storage; it gave standing; and Mrs. Forsyth fearlessly chanced acquaintance with these mothers, who would sometimes be there whole long mornings or afternoons, taking trunks out or putting them in. With the trunks set into the corridors and opened for them, they would spend the hours looking the contents over, talking to their neighbors, or rapt in long silences when they hesitated with things held off or up, and, after gazing absently at them, putting them back again. Sometimes they varied the process by laying things aside for sending home, and receipting for them at the office as "goods selected."

They were mostly hotel people or apartment people, as Mrs. Forsyth oftenest was herself, but sometimes they were separate-house people. Among these there was one family, not of great rank or wealth, but distinguished, as lifelong New-Yorkers, in a world of comers and goers of every origin. Mrs. Forsyth especially liked them for a certain quality, but what this quality was she could not very well say. They were a mother with two daughters, not quite old maids, but on the way to it, and there was very intermittently the apparently bachelor brother of the girls; at the office Mrs. Forsyth verified her conjecture that he was some sort of minister. One could see they were all gentlefolks, though the girls were not of the last cry of fashion. They were very nice to their mother, and you could tell that they must have been coming with her for years.

At this point in her study of them for her husband's amusement she realized that Charlotte had been coming to the storage with her nearly all her life, and that more and more the child had taken charge of the uneventful inspection of the things. She was shocked to think that she had let this happen, and now she commanded her husband to say whether Charlotte would grow into a storage old maid like those good girls.

Forsyth said, Probably not before her time; but he allowed it was a point to be considered.

Very well, then, Mrs. Forsyth said, the child should never go again; that was all. She had strongly confirmed herself in this resolution when one day she not only let the child go again, but she let her go alone. The child was now between seventeen and eighteen, rather tall, grave, pretty, with the dull brown hair that goes so well with dreaming blue eyes, and of a stiff grace. She had not come out yet, because she had always been out, handing cakes at her father's studio teas long before she could remember not doing it, and later pouring for her mother with rather a quelling air as she got toward fifteen. During these years the family had been going and coming between Europe and America; they did not know perfectly why, except that it was easier than not.

More and more there was a peculiarity in the goods selected by Charlotte for sending home, which her mother one day noted. "How is it, Charlotte, that you always send exactly the things I want, and when you get your own things here you don't know whether they are what you wanted or not?"

"Because I don't know when I send them. I don't choose them; I can't."

"But you choose the right things for me?"

"No, I don't, mother. I just take what comes first, and you always like it."

"Now, that is nonsense, Charlotte. I can't have you telling me such a thing as that. It's an insult to my intelligence. Do you think I don't know my own mind?"

"I don't know my mind," the girl said, so persistently, obstinately, stubbornly, that her mother did not pursue the subject for fear of worse.

She referred it to her husband, who said: "Perhaps it's like poets never being able to remember their own poetry. I've heard it's because they have several versions in their minds when they write and can't remember which they've written. Charlotte has several choices in her mind, and can't choose between her choices."

"Well, we ought to have broken her of her indecision. Some day it will make her very unhappy."

"Pretty hard to break a person of her temperament," Forsyth suggested.

"I know it!" his wife admitted, with a certain pleasure in realizing the fact. "I don't know what we shall do."

III

Storage society was almost wholly feminine; in rare instances there was a man who must have been sent in dearth of women or in an hour of their disability. Then the man came hastily, with a porter, and either pulled all the things out of the rooms so that he could honestly say he had seen them, and that the thing wanted was not there; or else merely had the doors opened, and after a glance inside resolved to wait till his wife, or mother, or daughter could come. He agreed in guilty eagerness with the workmen that this was the only way.

The exception to the general rule was a young man who came one bright spring morning when all nature suggested getting one's stuff out and going into the country, and had the room next the Forsyths' original five-dollar room opened. As it happened, Charlotte was at the moment visiting this room upon her mother's charge to see whether certain old scrim sash-curtains, which they had not needed for ages but at last simply must have, were not lurking there in a chest of general curtainings. The Forsyths now had rooms on other floors, but their main room was at the end of the corridor branching northward from that where the five-dollar room was. Near this main room that nice New York family had their rooms, and Charlotte had begun the morning in their friendly neighborhood, going through some chests that might perhaps have the general curtainings in them and the scrim curtains among the rest. It had not, and she had gone to what the Forsyths called their old ancestral five-dollar room, where that New York family continued to project a sort of wireless chaperonage over her. But the young man had come with a porter, and, with her own porter, Charlotte could not feel that even a wireless chaperonage was needed, though the young man approached with the most beaming face she thought she had ever seen, and said he hoped he should not be in her way. She answered with a sort of helpless reverberation of his glow, Not at all; she should only be a moment. She wanted to say she hoped she would not be in his way, but she saved herself in time, while, with her own eyes intent upon the façade of her room and her mind trying to lose itself in the question which curtain-trunk the scrims might be in, she kept the sense of his sweet eyes, the merriest eyes she had ever seen, effulgent with good-will and apology and reverent admiration. She blushed to think it admiration, though she liked to think it so, and she did not snub him when the young man jumped about, neglecting his own storage, and divining the right moments for his offers of help. She saw that he was a little shorter than herself, that he was very light and quick on his feet, and had a round, brown face, clean-shaven, and a round, brown head, close shorn, from which in the zeal of his attentions to her he had shed his straw hat onto the window-sill. He formed a strong contrast to the contents of his store-room, which was full, mainly, of massive white furniture picked out in gold, and very blond. He said casually that it had been there, off and on, since long before he could remember, and at these words an impression, vague, inexplicable, deepened in Charlotte's mind.

"Mother," she said, for she had now disused the earlier "mamma" in deference to modern usage, "how old was I when we first took that five-dollar room?"

She asked this question after she had shown the scrim curtains she had found and brought home with her.

"Why? I don't know. Two or three; three or four. I should have to count up. What makes you ask?"

"Can a person recollect what happened when they were three or four?"

"I should say not, decidedly."

"Or recollect a face?"

"Certainly not."

"Then of course it wasn't. Mother, do you remember ever telling me what the little boy was like who gave me all his playthings and I couldn't decide what to give him back?"

"What a question! Of course not! He was very brown and funny, with the beamingest little face in the world. Rather short for his age, I should say, though I haven't the least idea what his age was."

"Then it was the very same little boy!" Charlotte said.

"Who was the very same little boy?" her mother demanded.

"The one that was there to-day; the young man, I mean," Charlotte explained, and then she told what had happened with a want of fullness which her mother's imagination supplied.

"Did he say who he was? Is he coming back to-morrow or this afternoon? Did you inquire who he was or where?"

"What an idea, mother!" Charlotte said, grouping the several impossibilities under one head in her answer.

"You had a perfect right to know, if you thought he was the one."

"But I didn't think he was the one, and I don't know that he is now; and if he was, what could I do about it?"

"That is true," Mrs. Forsyth owned. "But it's very disappointing. I've always felt as if they ought to know it was your undecidedness and not ungenerousness."

Charlotte laughed a little forlornly, but she only said, "Really, mother!"

Mrs. Forsyth was still looking at the curtains. "Well, these are not the scrims I wanted. You must go back. I believe I will go with you. The sooner we have it over the better," she added, and she left the undecided Charlotte to decide whether she meant the scrim curtains or the young man's identity.

It was very well, for one reason, that she decided to go with Charlotte that afternoon. The New-Yorkers must have completed the inspection of their trunks, for they had not come back. Their failure to do so was the more important because the young man had come back and was actively superintending the unpacking of his room. The palatial furniture had all been ranged up and down the corridor, and as fast as a trunk was got out and unlocked he went through it with the help of the storage-men, listed its contents in a note-book with a number, and then transferred the number and a synopsis of the record to a tag and fastened it to the trunk, which he had put back into the room.

When the Forsyths arrived with the mistaken scrim curtains, he interrupted himself with apologies for possibly being in their way; and when Mrs. Forsyth said he was not at all in their way, he got white-and-gold arm-chairs for her and Charlotte and put them so conveniently near the old ancestral room that Mrs. Forsyth scarcely needed to move hand or foot in letting Charlotte restore the wrong curtains and search the chests for the right ones. His politeness made way for conversation and for the almost instant exchange of confidences between himself and Mrs. Forsyth, so that Charlotte was free to enjoy the silence to which they left her in her labors.

"Before I say a word," Mrs. Forsyth said, after saying some hundreds in their mutual inculpation and exculpation, "I want to ask something, and I hope you will excuse it to an old woman's curiosity and not think it rude."

At the words "old woman's" the young man gave a protesting "Oh!" and at the word "rude" he said, "Not at all."

"It is simply this: how long have your things been here? I ask because we've had this room thirteen or fourteen years, and I've never seen your room opened in that whole time."

The young man laughed joyously. "Because it hasn't been opened in that whole time. I was a little chap of three or four bothering round here when my mother put the things in; I believe it was a great frolic for me, but I'm afraid it wasn't for her. I've been told that my activities contributed to the confusion of the things and the things in them that she's been in ever since, and I'm here now to make what reparation I can by listing them."

"She'll find it a great blessing," Mrs. Forsyth said. "I wish we had ours listed. I suppose you remember it all very vividly. It must have been a great occasion for you seeing the things stored at that age."

The young man beamed upon her. "Not so great as now, I'm afraid. The fact is, I don't remember anything about it. But I've been told that I embarrassed with my personal riches a little girl who was looking over her doll's things."

"Oh, indeed!" Mrs. Forsyth said, stiffly, and she turned rather snubbingly from him and said, coldly, to Charlotte: "I think they are in that green trunk. Have you the key?" and, stooping as her daughter stooped, she whispered, "Really!" in condemnation and contempt.

Charlotte showed no signs of sharing either, and Mrs. Forsyth could not very well manage them alone. So when Charlotte said, "No, I haven't the key, mother," and the young man burst in with, "Oh, do let me try my master-key; it will unlock anything that isn't a Yale," Mrs. Forsyth sank back enthroned and the trunk was thrown open.

She then forgot what she had wanted it opened for. Charlotte said, "They're not here, mother," and her mother said, "No, I didn't suppose they were," and began to ask the young man about his mother. It appeared that his father had died twelve years before, and since then his mother and he had been nearly everywhere except at home, though mostly in England; now they had come home to see where they should go next or whether they should stay.

"That would never suit my daughter," Mrs. Forsyth lugged in, partly because the talk had gone on away from her family as long as she could endure, and partly because Charlotte's indecision always amused her. "She can't bear to choose."

"Really?" the young man said. "I don't know whether I like it or not, but I have had to do a lot of it. You mustn't think, though, that I chose this magnificent furniture. My father bought an Italian palace once, and as we couldn't live in it or move it we brought the furniture here."

"It is magnificent," Mrs. Forsyth said, looking down the long stretches of it and eying and fingering her specific throne. "I wish my husband could see it—I don't believe he remembers it from fourteen years ago. It looks—excuse me!—very studio."

"Is he a painter? Not Mr. Forsyth the painter?"

"Yes," Mrs. Forsyth eagerly admitted, but wondering how he should know her name, without reflecting that a score of trunk-tags proclaimed it and that she had acquired his by like means.

"I like his things so much," he said. "I thought his three portraits were the best things in the Salon last year."

"Oh, you saw them?" Mrs. Forsyth laughed with pleasure and pride. "Then," as if it necessarily followed, "you must come to us some Sunday afternoon. You'll find a number of his new portraits and some of the subjects; they like to see themselves framed." She tried for a card in her hand-bag, but she had none, and she said, "Have you one of my cards, my dear?" Charlotte had, and rendered it up with a severity lost upon her for the moment. She held it toward him. "It's Mr. Peter Bream?" she smiled upon him, and he beamed back.

"Did you remember it from our first meeting?"

In their cab Mrs. Forsyth said, "I don't know whether he's what you call rather fresh or not, Charlotte, and I'm not sure that I've been very wise. But he is so nice, and he looked so glad to be asked."

Charlotte did not reply at once, and her silent severity came to the surface of her mother's consciousness so painfully that it was rather a relief to have her explode, "Mother, I will thank you not to discuss my temperament with people."

She gave Mrs. Forsyth her chance, and her mother was so happy in being able to say, "I won't—your temper, my dear," that she could add with sincere apology: "I'm sorry I vexed you, and I won't do it again."

IV

The next day was Sunday; Peter Bream took it for some Sunday, and came to the tea on Mrs. Forsyth's generalized invitation. She pulled her mouth down and her eyebrows up when his card was brought in, but as he followed hard she made a lightning change to a smile and gave him a hand of cordial welcome. Charlotte had no choice but to welcome him, too, and so the matter was simple for her. She was pouring, as usual, for her mother, who liked to eliminate herself from set duties and walk round among the actual portraits in fact and in frame and talk about them to the potential portraits. Peter, qualified by long sojourn in England, at once pressed himself into the service of handing about the curate's assistant; Mrs. Forsyth electrically explained that it was one of the first brought to New York, and that she had got it at the Stores in London fifteen years before, and it had often been in the old ancestral room, and was there on top of the trunks that first day. She did not recur to the famous instance of Charlotte's infant indecision, and Peter was safe from a snub when he sat down by the girl's side and began to make her laugh. At the end, when her mother asked Charlotte what they had been laughing about, she could not tell; she said she did not know they were laughing.

The next morning Mrs. Forsyth was paying for her Sunday tea with a Monday headache, and more things must be got out for the country. Charlotte had again no choice but to go alone to the storage, and yet again no choice but to be pleasant to Peter when she found him next door listing the contents of his mother's trunks and tagging them as before. He dropped his work and wanted to help her. Suddenly they seemed strangely well acquainted, and he pretended to be asked which pieces she should put aside as goods selected, and chose them for her. She hinted that he was shirking his own work; he said it was an all-summer's job, but he knew her mother was in a hurry. He found the little old trunk of her playthings, and got it down and opened it and took out some toys as goods selected. She made him put them back, but first he catalogued everything in it and synopsized the list on a tag and tagged the trunk. He begged for a broken doll which he had not listed, and Charlotte had so much of her original childish difficulty in parting with that instead of something else that she refused it.

It came lunch-time, and he invited her to go out to lunch with him; and when she declined with dignity he argued that if they went to the Woman's Exchange she would be properly chaperoned by the genius of the place; besides, it was the only place in town where you got real strawberry shortcake. She was ashamed of liking it all; he besought her to let him carry her hand-bag for her, and, as he already had it, she could not prevent him; she did not know, really, how far she might successfully forbid him in anything. At the street door of the apartment-house they found her mother getting out of a cab, and she asked Peter in to lunch; so that Charlotte might as well have lunched with him at the Woman's Exchange.

At all storage warehouses there is a season in autumn when the corridors are heaped with the incoming furniture of people who have decided that they cannot pass another winter in New York and are breaking up housekeeping to go abroad indefinitely. But in the spring, when the Constitutional Safe-Deposit offered ample space for thoughtful research, the meetings of Charlotte and Peter could recur without more consciousness of the advance they were making toward the fated issue than in so many encounters at tea or luncheon or dinner. Mrs. Forsyth was insisting on rather a drastic overhauling of her storage that year. Some of the things, by her command, were shifted to and fro between the more modern rooms and the old ancestral room, and Charlotte had to verify the removals. In deciding upon goods selected for the country she had the help of Peter, and she helped him by interposing some useful hesitations in the case of things he had put aside from his mother's possessions to be sold for her by the warehouse people.

One day he came late and told Charlotte that his mother had suddenly taken her passage for England, and they were sailing the next morning. He said, as if it logically followed, that he had been in love with her from that earliest time when she would not give him the least of her possessions, and now he asked her if she would not promise him the greatest. She did not like what she felt "rehearsed" in his proposal; it was not her idea of a proposal, which ought to be spontaneous and unpremeditated in terms; at the same time, she resented his precipitation, which she could not deny was inevitable.

She perceived that they were sitting side by side on two of those white-and-gold thrones, and she summoned an indignation with the absurdity in refusing him. She rose and said that she must go; that she must be going; that it was quite time for her to go; and she would not let him follow her to the elevator, as he made some offer of doing, but left him standing among his palatial furniture like a prince in exile.

By the time she reached home she had been able to decide that she must tell her mother at once. Her mother received the fact of Peter's proposal with such transport that she did not realize the fact of Charlotte's refusal. When this was connoted to her she could scarcely keep her temper within the bounds of maternal tenderness. She said she would have nothing more to do with such a girl; that there was but one such pearl as Peter in the universe, and for Charlotte to throw him away like that! Was it because she could not decide? Well, it appeared that she could decide wrong quickly enough when it came to the point. Would she leave it now to her mother?

That Charlotte would not do, but what she did do was to write a letter to Peter taking him back as much as rested with her; but delaying so long in posting it, when it was written, that it reached him among the letters sent on board and supplementarily delivered by his room steward after all the others when the ship had sailed. The best Peter could do in response was a jubilant Marconigram of unequaled cost and comprehensiveness.

His mother had meant to return in the fall, after her custom, to find out whether she wished to spend the winter in New York or not. Before the date for her sailing she fell sick, and Peter came sadly home alone in the spring. Mrs. Bream's death brought Mrs. Forsyth a vain regret; she was sorry now that she had seen so little of Mrs. Bream; Peter's affection for her was beautiful and spoke worlds for both of them; and they, the Forsyths, must do what they could to comfort him.

Charlotte felt the pathos of his case peculiarly when she went to make provision for goods selected for the summer from the old ancestral room, and found him forlorn among his white-and-gold furniture next door. He complained that he had no association with it except the touching fact of his mother's helplessness with it, which he had now inherited. The contents of the trunks were even less intimately of his experience; he had performed a filial duty in listing their contents, which long antedated him, and consisted mostly of palatial bric-à-brac and the varied spoils of travel.

He cheered up, however, in proposing to her that they should buy a Castle in Spain and put them into it. The fancy pleased her, but visibly she shrank from a step which it involved, so that he was, as it were, forced to say, half jokingly, half ruefully, "I can imagine your not caring for this rubbish or what became of it, Charlotte, but what about the owner?"

"The owner?" she asked, as it were somnambulantly.

"Yes. Marrying him, say, sometime soon."

"Oh, Peter, I couldn't."

"Couldn't? You know that's not playing the game exactly."

"Yes; but not—not right away?"

"Well, I don't know much about it in my own case, but isn't it usual to fix some approximate date? When should you think?"

"Oh, Peter, I can't think."

"Will you let me fix it? I must go West and sell out and pull up, you know, preparatory to never going again. We can fix the day now or we can fix it when I come back."

"Oh, when you come back," she entreated so eagerly that Peter said:

"Charlotte, let me ask you one thing. Were you ever sorry you wrote me that taking-back letter?"

"Why, Peter, you know how I am. When I have decided something I have undecided it. That's all."

From gay he turned to grave. "I ought to have thought. I haven't been fair; I haven't played the game. I ought to have given you another chance; and I haven't, have I?"

"Why, I suppose a girl can always change," Charlotte said, suggestively.

"Yes, but you won't always be a girl. I've never asked you if you wanted to change. I ask you now. Do you?"

"How can I tell? Hadn't we better let it go as it is? Only not hurry about—about—marrying?"

"Certainly not hurry about marrying. I've wondered that a girl could make up her mind to marry any given man. Haven't you ever wished that you had not made up your mind about me?"

"Hundreds of times. But I don't know that I meant anything by it."

He took her hand from where it lay in her lap as again she sat on one of the white-and-gold thrones beside him and gently pressed it. "Well, then, let's play we have never been engaged. I'm going West to-night to settle things up for good, and I won't be back for three or four months, and when I come back we'll start new. I'll ask you, and you shall say yes or no just as if you had never said either before."

"Peter, when you talk like that!" She saw his brown, round face dimly through her wet eyes, and she wanted to hug him for pity of him and pride in him, but she could not decide to do it. They went out to lunch at the Woman's Exchange, and the only regret Peter had was that it was so long past the season of strawberry shortcake, and that Charlotte seemed neither to talk nor to listen; she ought to have done one or the other.

They had left the Vaneckens busy with their summer trunks at the far end of the northward corridor, where their wireless station had been re-established for Charlotte's advantage, though she had not thought of it the whole short morning long. When she came back from lunch the Vaneckens were just brushing away the crumbs of theirs, which the son and brother seemed to have brought in for them in a paper box; at any rate, he was now there, making believe to help them.

Mrs. Forsyth had promised to come, but she came so late in the afternoon that she owned she had been grudgingly admitted at the office, and she was rather indignant about it. By this time, without having been West for three months, Peter had asked a question which had apparently never been asked before, and Charlotte had as newly answered it. "And now, mother," she said, while Mrs. Forsyth passed from indignant to exultant, "I want to be married right away, before Peter changes his mind about taking me West with him. Let us go home at once. You always said I should have a home wedding."

"What a ridiculous idea!" Mrs. Forsyth said, more to gain time than anything else. She added, "Everything is at sixes and sevens in the flat. There wouldn't be standing-room." A sudden thought flashed upon her, which, because it was sudden and in keeping with her character, she put into tentative words. "You're more at home here than anywhere else. You were almost born here. You've played about here ever since you were a child. You first met Peter here. He proposed to you here, and you rejected him here. He's proposed here again, and you've accepted him, you say—"

"Mother!" Charlotte broke in terribly upon her. "Are you suggesting that I should be married in a storage warehouse? Well, I haven't fallen quite so low as that yet. If I can't have a home wedding, I will have a church wedding, and I will wait till doomsday for it if necessary."

"I don't know about doomsday," Mrs. Forsyth said, "but as far as to-day is concerned, it's too late for a church wedding. Peter, isn't there something about canonical hours? And isn't it past them?"

"That's in the Episcopal Church," Peter said, and then he asked, very politely, "Will you excuse me for a moment?" and walked away as if he had an idea. It was apparently to join the Vaneckens, who stood in a group at the end of their corridor, watching the restoration of the trunks which they had been working over the whole day. He came back with Mr. Vanecken and Mr. Vanecken's mother. He was smiling radiantly, and they amusedly.

"It's all right," he explained. "Mr. Vanecken is a Presbyterian minister, and he will marry us now."

"But not here!" Charlotte cried, feeling herself weaken.

"No, certainly not," the dominie reassured her. "I know a church in the next block that I can borrow for the occasion. But what about the license?"

It was in the day before the parties must both make application in person, and Peter took a paper from his breast pocket. "I thought it might be needed, sometime, and I got it on the way up, this morning."

"Oh, how thoughtful of you, Peter!" Mrs. Forsyth moaned in admiration otherwise inexpressible, and the rest laughed, even Charlotte, who laughed hysterically. At the end of the corridor they met the Misses Vanecken waiting for them, unobtrusively expectant, and they all went down in the elevator together. Just as they were leaving the building, which had the air of hurrying them out, Mrs. Forsyth had an inspiration. "Good heavens!" she exclaimed, and then, in deference to Mr. Vanecken, said, "Good gracious, I mean. My husband! Peter, go right into the office and telephone Mr. Forsyth."

"Perhaps," Mr. Vanecken said, "I had better go and see about having my friend's church opened, in the meanwhile, and—"

"By all means!" Mrs. Forsyth said from her mood of universal approbation.

But Mr. Vanecken came back looking rather queer and crestfallen. "I find my friend has gone into the country for a few days; and I don't quite like to get the sexton to open the church without his authority, and— But New York is full of churches, and we can easily find another, with a little delay, if—"

He looked at Peter, who looked at Charlotte, who burst out with unprecedented determination. "No, we can't wait. I shall never marry Peter if we do. Mother, you are right. But must it be in the old ancestral five-dollar room?"

They all laughed except Charlotte, who was more like crying.

"Certainly not," Mr. Vanecken said. "I've no doubt the manager—"

He never seemed to end his sentences, and he now left this one broken off while he penetrated the railing which fenced in the manager alone among a group of vacated desks, frowning impatient. At some murmured words from the dominie, he shouted, "What!" and then came out radiantly smiling, and saying, "Why, certainly." He knew all the group as old storers in the Constitutional, and called them each by name as he shook them each by the hand. "Everything else has happened here, and I don't see why this shouldn't. Come right into the reception-room."

With some paintings of biblical subjects, unclaimed from the storage, on the walls, the place had a religious effect, and the manager significantly looked out of it a lingering stenographer, who was standing before a glass with two hatpins crossed in her mouth preparatory to thrusting them through the straw. She withdrew, visibly curious and reluctant, and then the manager offered to withdraw himself.

"No," Charlotte said, surprisingly initiative in these junctures, "I don't know how it is in Mr. Vanecken's church, but, if father doesn't come, perhaps you'll have to give me away. At any rate, you're an old friend of the family, and I should be hurt if you didn't stay."

She laid her hand on the manager's arm, and just as he had protestingly and politely consented, her father arrived in a taxicab, rather grumbling from having been obliged to cut short a sitting. When it was all over, and the Vaneckens were eliminated, when, in fact, the Breams had joined the Forsyths at a wedding dinner which the bride's father had given them at Delmonico's and had precipitated themselves into a train for Niagara ("So banal," Mrs. Forsyth said, "but I suppose they had to go somewhere, and we went to Niagara, come to think of it, and it's on their way West"), the bride's mother remained up late talking it all over. She took credit to herself for the whole affair, and gave herself a great deal of just praise. But when she said, "I do believe, if it hadn't been for me, at the last, Charlotte would never have made up her mind," Forsyth demurred.

"I should say Peter had a good deal to do with making up her mind for her."

"Yes, you might say that."

"And for once in her life Charlotte seems to have had her mind ready for making up."

"Yes, you might say that, too. I believe she is going to turn out a decided character, after all. I never saw anybody so determined not to be married in a storage warehouse."

A PRESENTIMENT

Over our coffee in the Turkish room Minver was usually a censor of our several foibles rather than a sharer in our philosophic speculations and metaphysical conjectures. He liked to disable me as one professionally vowed to the fabulous, and he had unfailing fun with the romantic sentimentality of Rulledge, which was in fact so little in keeping with the gross super-abundance of his person, his habitual gluttony, and his ridiculous indolence. Minver knew very well that Rulledge was a good fellow withal, and would willingly do any kind action that did not seriously interfere with his comfort, or make too heavy a draft upon his pocket. His self-indulgence, which was quite blameless, unless surfeit is a fault, was the basis of an interest in occult themes, which was the means of even higher diversion to Minver. He liked to have Rulledge approach Wanhope from this side, in the invincible persuasion that the psychologist would be interested in these themes by the law of his science, though he had been assured again and again that in spite of its misleading name psychology did not deal with the soul as Rulledge supposed the soul; and Minver's eyes lighted up with a prescience of uncommon pleasure when, late one night, after we had vainly tried to hit it off in talk, now of this, now of that, Rulledge asked Wanhope, abruptly as if it followed from something before:

"Wasn't there a great deal more said about presentiments forty or fifty years ago than there is now?"

Wanhope had been lapsing deeper and deeper into the hollow of his chair; but he now pulled himself up, and turned quickly toward Rulledge. "What made you think of that?" he asked.

"I don't know. Why?"

"Because I was thinking of it myself." He glanced at me, and I shook my head.

"Well," Minver said, "if it will leave Acton out in the cold, I'll own that I was thinking of it, too. I was going back in my mind, for no reason that I know of, to my childhood, when I first heard of such a thing as a presentiment, and when I was afraid of having one. I had the notion that presentiments ran in the family."

"Why had you that notion?" Rulledge demanded.

"I don't know that I proposed telling," the painter said, giving himself to his pipe.

"Perhaps you didn't have it," Rulledge retaliated.

"Perhaps," Minver assented.

Wanhope turned from the personal aspect of the matter. "It's rather curious that we should all three have had the same thing in mind just now; or, rather, it is not very curious. Such coincidences are really very common. Something must have been said at dinner which suggested it to all of us."

"All but Acton," Minver demurred.

"I mightn't have heard what was said," I explained. "I suppose the passing of all that sort of sub-beliefs must date from the general lapse of faith in personal immortality."

"Yes, no doubt," Wanhope assented. "It is very striking how sudden the lapse was. Everyone who experienced it in himself could date it to a year, if not to a day. The agnosticism of scientific men was of course all the time undermining the fabric of faith, and then it fell in abruptly, reaching one believer after another as fast as the ground was taken wholly or partly from under his feet. I can remember how people once disputed whether there were such beings as guardian spirits or not. That minor question was disposed of when it was decided that there were no spirits at all."

"Naturally," Minver said. "And the decay of the presentiment must have been hastened by the failure of so many presentiments to make good."

"The great majority of them have failed to make good, from the beginning of time," Wanhope replied.

"There are two kinds of presentiments," Rulledge suggested, with a philosophic air. "The true and the untrue."

"Like mushrooms," Minver said. "Only, the true presentiment kills, and the true mushroom nourishes. Talking of mushrooms, they have a way in Switzerland of preserving them in walnut oil, and they fill you with the darkest forebodings, after you've filled yourself with the mushrooms. There's some occult relation between the two. Think it out, Rulledge!"

Rulledge ignored him in turning to Wanhope. "The trouble is how to distinguish the true from the untrue presentiment."

"It would be interesting," Wanhope began, but Minver broke in upon him maliciously.

"To know how much the dyspepsia of our predecessors had to with the prevalence of presentimentalism? I agree with you, that a better diet has a good deal to do with the decline of the dark foreboding among us. What I can't understand is, how a gross and reckless feeder, like Rulledge here, doesn't go about like ancestral voices prophesying all sorts of dreadful things."

"That's rather cheap talk, even for you, Minver," Rulledge said. "Why did you think presentiments ran in your family?"

"Well, there you have me, Rulledge. That's where my theory fails. I can remember," Minver continued soberly, "the talk there used to be about them among my people. They were serious people in an unreligious way, or rather an unecclesiastical way. They were never spiritualists, but I don't think there was one of them who doubted that he should live hereafter; he might doubt that he was living here, but there was no question of the other thing. I must say it gave a dignity to their conversation which, when they met, as they were apt to do at one another's houses on Sunday nights, was not of common things. One of my uncles was a merchant, another a doctor; my father was a portrait-painter by profession, and a sign-painter by practice. I suppose that's where I got my knack, such as it is. The merchant was an invalid, rather, though he kept about his business, and our people merely recognized him as being out of health. He was what we could call, for that day and region—the Middle West of the early fifties—a man of unusual refinement. I suppose this was temperamental with him largely; but he had cultivated tastes, too. I remember him as a peculiarly gentle person, with a pensive cast of face, and the melancholy accomplishment of playing the flute."

"I wonder why nobody plays the flute nowadays," I mused aloud.

"Yes, it's quite obsolete," Minver said. "They only play the flute in the orchestras now. I always look at the man who plays it and think of my uncle. He used to be very nice to me as a child; and he was very fond of my father, in a sort of filial way; my father was so much older. I can remember my young aunt; and how pretty she was as she sat at the piano, and sang and played to his fluting. When she looked forward at the music, her curls fell into her neck; they wore curls then, grown-up women; and though I don't think curls are beautiful, my aunt's beauty would have been less without them; in fact, I can't think of her without them.

"She was delicate, too; they were really a pair of invalids; but she had none of his melancholy. They had had several children, who died, one after another, and there was only one left at the time I am speaking of. I rather wonder, now, that the thought of those poor little ghost-cousins didn't make me uncomfortable. I was a very superstitious boy, but I seem not to have thought of them. I played with the little girl who was left, and I liked going to my uncle's better than anywhere else. I preferred going in the daytime and in the summer-time. Then my cousin and I sat in a nook of the garden and fought violets, as we called it; hooked the wry necks of the flowers together and twitched to see which blossom would come off first. She was a sunny little thing, like her mother, and she had curls, like her. I can't express the feeling I had for my aunt; she seemed the embodiment of a world that was at once very proud and very good. I suppose she dressed fashionably, as things went then and there; and her style as well as her beauty fascinated me. I would have done anything to please her, far more than to please my cousin. With her I used to squabble, and sometimes sent her crying to her mother. Then I always ran off home, but when I sneaked back, or was sent for to come and play with my cousin, I was not scolded for my wickedness.

"My uncle was more prosperous than his brothers; he lived in a much better house than ours, and I used to be quite awe-struck by its magnificence. He went East, as we said, twice a year to buy goods, and he had things sent back for his house such as we never saw elsewhere; those cask-shaped seats of blue china for the verandas, and bamboo chairs. There were cane-bottom chairs in the sitting-room, such as we had in our best room; in the parlor the large pieces were of mahogany veneer, upholstered in black hair-cloth; they held me in awe. The piano filled half the place; the windows came down to the ground, and had Venetian blinds and lace curtains.

"We all went in there after the Sunday night supper, and then the fathers and mothers were apt to begin talking of those occult things that gave me the creeps. It was after the Rochester Knockings, as they were called, had been exposed, and so had spread like an infection everywhere. It was as if people were waiting to have the fraud shown up in order to believe in it."

"That sort of thing happens," Wanhope agreed. "It's as if the seeds of the ventilated imposture were carried atmospherically into the human mind broadcast and a universal crop of self-delusion sprang up."

"At any rate," Minver resumed, "instead of the gift being confined to a few persons—a small sisterhood with detonating knee-joints—there were rappings in every well-regulated household; all the tables tipped; people went to sleep to the soft patter of raps on the headboards of their beds; and girls who could not spell were occupied in delivering messages from Socrates, Ben Franklin and Shakespeare. Besides the physical demonstrations, there were all sorts of psychical intimations from the world which we've now abolished."

"Not permanently, perhaps," I suggested.

"Well, that remains to be seen," Minver said. "It was this sort of thing which my people valued above the other. Perhaps they were exclusive in their tastes, and did not care for an occultism which the crowd could share with them; though this is a conjecture too long after the fact to have much value. As far as I can now remember, they used to talk of the double presence of living persons, like their being where they greatly wished to be as well as where they really were; of clairvoyance; of what we call mind-transference, now; of weird coincidences of all kinds; of strange experiences of their own and of others; of the participation of animals in these experiences, like the testimony of cats and dogs to the presence of invisible spirits; of dreams that came true, or came near coming true; and, above everything, of forebodings and presentiments.

"I dare say they didn't always talk of such things, and I'm giving possibly a general impression from a single instance; everything remembered of childhood is as if from large and repeated occurrence. But it must have happened more than once, for I recall that when it came to presentiments my aunt broke it up, perhaps once only. My cousin used to get very sleepy on the rug before the fire, and her mother would carry her off to bed, very cross and impatient of being kissed good night, while I was left to the brunt of the occult alone. I could not go with my aunt and cousin, and I folded myself in my mother's skirt, where I sat at her feet, and listened in an anguish of drowsy terror. The talk would pass into my dreams, and the dreams would return into the talk; and I would suffer a sort of double nightmare, waking and sleeping."

"Poor little devil!" Rulledge broke out. "It's astonishing how people will go on before children, and never think of the misery they're making for them."

"I believe my mother thought of it," Minver returned, "but when that sort of talk began, the witchery of it was probably too strong for her. 'It held her like a two years' child'; I was eight that winter. I don't know how long my suffering had gone on, when my aunt came back and seemed to break up the talk. It had got to presentiments, and, whether they knew that this was forbidden ground with her, or whether she now actually said something about it, they turned to talk of other things. I'm not telling you all this from my own memory, which deals with only a point or two. My father and mother used to recur to it when I was older, and I am piecing out my story from their memories.

"My uncle, with all his temperamental pensiveness, was my aunt's stay and cheer in the fits of depression which she paid with for her usual gaiety. But these fits always began with some uncommon depression of his—some effect of the forebodings he was subject to. Her opposition to that kind of thing was purely unselfish, but certainly she dreaded it for him as well as herself. I suppose there was a sort of conscious silence in the others which betrayed them to her. 'Well,' she said, laughing, 'have you been at it again? That poor child looks frightened out of his wits.'

"They all laughed then, and my father said, hypocritically, 'I was just going to ask Felix whether he expected to start East this week or next.'

"My uncle tried to make light of what was always a heavy matter with him. 'Well, yesterday,' he answered, 'I should have said next week; but it's this week, now. I'm going on Wednesday.'

"'By stage or packet?' my father asked.

"'Oh, I shall take the canal to the lake, and get the boat for Buffalo there,' my uncle said.

"They went on to speak of the trip to New York, and how much easier it was then than it used to be when you had to go by stage over the mountains to Philadelphia and on by stage again. Now, it seemed, you got the Erie Canal packet at Buffalo and the Hudson River steamboat at Albany, and reached New York in four or five days, in great comfort without the least fatigue. They had all risen and my aunt had gone out with her sisters-in-law to help them get their wraps. When they returned, it seemed that they had been talking of the journey, too, for she said to my mother, laughing again, 'Well, Richard may think it's easy; but somehow Felix never expects to get home alive.'

"I don't think I ever heard my uncle laugh, but I can remember how he smiled at my aunt's laughing, as he put his hand on her shoulder; I thought it was somehow a very sad smile. On Wednesday I was allowed to go with my aunt and cousin to see him off on the packet, which came up from Cincinnati early in the morning; I had lain awake most of the night, and then nearly overslept myself, and then was at the canal in time. We made a gay parting for him, but when the boat started, and I was gloating on the three horses making up the tow-path at a spanking trot, under the snaky spirals of the driver's smacking whip-lash, I caught sight of my uncle standing on the deck and smiling that sad smile of his. My aunt was waving her handkerchief, but when she turned away she put it to her eyes.

"The rest of the story, such as it is, I know, almost to the very end, from what I heard my father and mother say from my uncle's report afterward. He told them that, when the boat started, the stress to stay was so strong upon him that if he had not been ashamed he would have jumped ashore and followed us home. He said that he could not analyze his feelings; it was not yet any definite foreboding, but simply a depression that seemed to crush him so that all his movements were leaden, when he turned at last, and went down to breakfast in the cabin below. The stress did not lighten with the little changes and chances of the voyage to the lake. He was never much given to making acquaintance with people, but now he found himself so absent-minded that he was aware of being sometimes spoken to by friendly strangers without replying until it was too late even to apologize. He was not only steeped in this gloom, but he had the constant distress of the effort he involuntarily made to trace it back to some cause or follow it forward to some consequence. He kept trying at this, with a mind so tensely bent to the mere horror that he could not for a moment strain away from it. He would very willingly have occupied himself with other things, but the anguish which the double action of his mind gave him was such that he could not bear the effort; all he could do was to abandon himself to his obsession. This would ease him only for a while, though, and then he would suffer the misery of trying in vain to escape from it.

"He thought he must be going mad, but insanity implied some definite delusion or hallucination, and, so far as he could make out, he had none. He was simply crushed by a nameless foreboding. Something dreadful was to happen, but this was all he felt; knowledge had no part in his condition. He could not say whether he slept during the two nights that passed before he reached Toledo, where he was to take the lake steamer for Buffalo. He wished to turn back again, but the relentless pressure which had kept him from turning back at the start was as strong as ever with him. He tried to give his presentiment direction by talking with the other passengers about a recent accident to a lake steamer, in which several hundred lives were lost; there had been a collision in rough weather, and one of the boats had gone down in a few minutes. There was a sort of relief in that, but the double action of the mind brought the same intolerable anguish again, and he settled back for refuge under the shadow of his impenetrable doom. This did not lift till he was well on his way from Albany to New York by the Hudson River. The canal-boat voyage from Buffalo to Albany had been as eventless as that to Toledo, and his lake steamer had reached Buffalo in safety, for which it had seemed as if those lost in the recent disaster had paid.

"He tried to pierce his heavy cloud by argument from the security in which he had traveled so far, but the very security had its hopelessness. If something had happened—some slight accident—to interrupt it, his reason, or his unreason, might have taken it for a sign that the obscure doom, whatever it was, had been averted.

"Up to this time he had not been able to connect his foreboding with anything definite, and he was not afraid for himself. He was simply without the formless hope that helps us on at every step, through good and bad, and it was a mortal peril, which he came through safely while scores of others were lost, that gave his presentiment direction. He had taken the day boat from Albany, and about the middle of the afternoon the boat, making way under a head-wind, took fire. The pilot immediately ran her ashore, and her passengers, those that had the courage for it, ran aft, and began jumping from the stern, but a great many women and children were burned. My uncle was one of the first of those who jumped, and he stood in the water, trying to save those who came after from drowning; it was not very deep. Some of the women lost courage for the leap, and some turned back into the flames, remembering children they had left behind. One poor creature stood hesitating wildly, and he called up to her to jump. At last she did so, almost into his arms, and then she clung about him as he helped her ashore. 'Oh,' she cried out between her sobs, 'if you have a wife and children at home, God will take you safe back to them; you have saved my life for my husband and little ones.' 'No,' he was conscious of saying, 'I shall never see my wife again,' and now his foreboding had the direction that it had wanted before.

"From that on he simply knew that he should not get home alive, and he waited resignedly for the time and form of his disaster. He had a sort of peace in that. He went about his business intelligently, and from habit carefully, but it was with a mechanical action of the mind, something, he imagined, like the mechanical action of his body in those organs which do their part without bidding from the will. He was only a few days in New York, but in the course of them he got several letters from his wife telling him that all was going well with her and their daughter. It was before the times when you can ask and answer questions by telegraph, and he started back, necessarily without having heard the latest news from home.

"He made the return trip in a sort of daze, talking, reading, eating, and sleeping in the calm certainty of doom, and only wondering how it would be fulfilled, and what hour of the night or day. But it is no use my eking this out; I heard it, as I say, when I was a child, and I am afraid that if I should try to give it with the full detail I should take to inventing particulars." Minver paused a moment, and then he said: "But there was one thing that impressed itself indelibly on my memory. My uncle got back perfectly safe and well."

"Oh!" Rulledge snorted in rude dissatisfaction.

"What was it impressed itself on your memory?" Wanhope asked, with scientific detachment from the story as a story.

Minver continued to address Wanhope, without regarding Rulledge. "My uncle told my father that some sort of psychical change, which he could not describe, but which he was as conscious of as if it were physical, took place within him as he came in sight of his house—"

"Yes," Wanhope prompted.

"He had driven down from the canal-packet in the old omnibus which used to meet passengers and distribute them at their destinations in town. All the way to his house he was still under the doom as regarded himself, but bewildered that he should be getting home safe and well, and he was refusing his escape, as it were, and then suddenly, at the sight of the familiar house, the change within him happened. He looked out of the omnibus window and saw a group of neighbors at his gate. As he got out of the omnibus, my father took him by the hand, as if to hold him back a moment. Then he said to my father, very quietly, 'You needn't tell me: my wife is dead.'"

There was an appreciable pause, in which we were all silent, and then Rulledge demanded, greedily, "And was she?"

"Really, Rulledge!" I could not help protesting.

Minver asked him, almost compassionately and with unwonted gentleness, as from the mood in which his reminiscence had left him: "You suspected a hoax? She had died suddenly the night before while she and my cousin were getting things ready to welcome my uncle home in the morning. I'm sorry you're disappointed," he added, getting back to his irony.

"Whatever," Rulledge pursued, "became of the little girl?"

"She died rather young; a great many years ago; and my uncle soon after her."

Rulledge went away without saying anything, but presently returned with the sandwich which he had apparently gone for, while Wanhope was remarking: "That want of definition in the presentiment at first, and then its determination in the new direction by, as it were, propinquity—it is all very curious. Possibly we shall some day discover a law in such matters."

Rulledge said: "How was it your boyhood was passed in the Middle West, Minver? I always thought you were a Bostonian."

"I was an adoptive Bostonian for a good while, until I decided to become a native New-Yorker, so that I could always be near to you, Rulledge. You can never know what a delicate satisfaction you are."

Minver laughed, and we were severally restored to the wonted relations which his story had interrupted.

CAPTAIN DUNLEVY'S LAST TRIP

It was against the law, in such case made and provided, Of the United States, but by the good will of the pilots That we would some of us climb to the pilot-house after our breakfast For a morning smoke, and find ourselves seats on the benching Under the windows, or in the worn-smooth arm-chairs. The pilot, Which one it was did not matter, would tilt his head round and say, "All right!" When he had seen who we were, and begin, or go on as from stopping In the midst of talk that was leading up to a story, Just before we came in, and the story, begun or beginning, Always began or ended with some one, or something or other, Having to do with the river. If one left the wheel to the other, Going off watch, he would say to his partner standing behind him With his hands stretched out for the spokes that were not given up yet, "Captain, you can tell them the thing I was going to tell them Better than I could, I reckon," and then the other would answer, "Well, I don't know as I feel so sure of that, captain," and having Recognized each other so by that courtesy title of captain Never officially failed of without offense among pilots, One would subside into Jim and into Jerry the other.

It was on these terms, at least, Captain Dunn relieved Captain Davis When we had settled ourselves one day to listen in comfort, After some psychological subtleties we had indulged in at breakfast Touching that weird experience every one knows when the senses Juggle the points of the compass out of true orientation, Changing the North to the South, and the East to the West. "Why, Jerry, what was it You was going to tell them?" "Oh, never you mind what it was, Jim. You tell them something else," and so Captain Davis submitted, While Captain Dunn, with a laugh, got away beyond reach of his protest. Then Captain Davis, with fitting, deprecatory preamble, Launched himself on a story that promised to be all a story Could be expected to be, when one of those women—you know them— Who interrupt on any occasion or none, interrupted, Pointed her hand, and asked, "Oh, what is that island there, captain?" "That one, ma'am?" He gave her the name, and then the woman persisted, "Don't say you know them all by sight!" "Yes, by sight or by feeling." "What do you mean by feeling?" "Why, just that by daylight we see them, And in the dark it's like as if somehow we felt them, I reckon. Every foot of the channel and change in it, wash-out and cave-in, Every bend and turn of it, every sand-bar and landmark, Every island, of course, we have got to see them, or feel them." "But if you don't?" "But we've got to." "But aren't you ever mistaken?" "Never the second time." "Now, what do you mean, Captain Davis? Never the second time." "Well, let me tell you a story. It's not the one I begun, but that island you asked about yonder Puts me in mind of it, happens to be the place where it happened, Three years ago. I suppose no man ever knew the Ohio Better than Captain Dunlevy, if any one else knew it like him. Man and boy he had been pretty much his whole life on the river: Cabin-boy first on a keelboat before the day of the steamboats, Back in the pioneer times; and watchman then on a steamboat; Then second mate, and then mate, and then pilot and captain and owner— But he was proudest, I reckon, of being about the best pilot On the Ohio. He knew it as well as he knew his own Bible, And I don't hardly believe that ever Captain Dunlevy Let a single day go by without reading a chapter."

While the pilot went on with his talk, and in regular, rhythmical motion Swayed from one side to the other before his wheel, and we listened, Certain typical facts of the picturesque life of the river Won their way to our consciousness as without help of our senses. It was along about the beginning of March, but already In the sleepy sunshine the budding maples and willows, Where they waded out in the shallow wash of the freshet, Showed the dull red and the yellow green of their blossoms and catkins, And in their tops the foremost flocks of blackbirds debated As to which they should colonize first. The indolent house-boats Loafing along the shore, sent up in silvery spirals Out of their kitchen pipes the smoke of their casual breakfasts. Once a wide tow of coal-barges, loaded clear down to the gunwales, Gave us the slack of the current, with proper formalities shouted By the hoarse-throated stern-wheeler that pushed the black barges before her, And as she passed us poured a foamy cascade from her paddles. Then, as a raft of logs, which the spread of the barges had hidden, River-wide, weltered in sight, with a sudden jump forward the pilot Dropped his whole weight on the spokes of the wheel just in time to escape it.

"Always give those fellows," he joked, "all the leeway they ask for; Worst kind of thing on the river you want your boat to run into. Where had I got about Captain Dunlevy? Oh yes, I remember. Well, when the railroads began to run away from the steamboats, Taking the carrying trade in the very edge of the water, It was all up with the old flush times, and Captain Dunlevy Had to climb down with the rest of us pilots till he was only Captain the same as any and every pilot is captain, Glad enough, too, to be getting his hundred and twenty-five dollars Through the months of the spring and fall while navigation was open. Never lowered himself, though, a bit from captain and owner, Knew his rights and yours, and never would thought of allowing Any such thing as a liberty from you or taking one with you. I had been his cub, and all that I knew of the river Captain Dunlevy had learnt me; and if you know what the feeling Is of a cub for the pilot that learns him the river, you'll trust me When I tell you I felt it the highest kind of an honor Having him for my partner; and when I came up to relieve him, One day, here at the wheel, and actu'lly thought that I found him Taking that island there on the left, I thought I was crazy. No, I couldn't believe my senses, and yet I couldn't endure it. Seeing him climb the spokes of the wheel to warp the Kanawha, With the biggest trip of passengers ever she carried, Round on the bar at the left that fairly stuck out of the water.

Well, as I said, he learnt me all that I knew of the river, And was I to learn him now which side to take of an island When I knew he knew it like his right hand from his left hand? My, but I hated to speak! It certainly seemed like my tongue clove, Like the Bible says, to the roof of my mouth! But I had to. 'Captain,' I says, and it seemed like another person was talking, 'Do you usu'lly take that island there on the eastward?' 'Yes,' he says, and he laughed, 'and I thought I had learnt you to do it, When you was going up.' 'But not going down, did you, captain?' 'Down?' And he whirled at me, and, without ever stopping his laughing, Turned as white as a sheet, and his eyes fairly bulged from their sockets. Then he whirled back again, and looked up and down on the river, Like he was hunting out the shape of the shore and the landmarks. Well, I suppose the thing has happened to every one sometime, When you find the points of the compass have swapped with each other, And at the instant you're looking, the North and the South have changed places. I knew what was in his mind as well as Dunlevy himself did. Neither one of us spoke a word for nearly a minute. Then in a kind of whisper he says, 'Take the wheel, Captain Davis!' Let the spokes fly, and while I made a jump forwards to catch them, Staggered into that chair—well, the very one you are in, ma'am. Set there breathing quick, and, when he could speak, all he said was, 'This is the end of it for me on the river, Jim Davis,' Reached up over his head for his coat where it hung by that window, Trembled onto his feet, and stopped in the door there a second, Stared in hard like as if for good-by to the things he was used to, Shut the door behind him, and never come back again through it." While we were silent, not liking to prompt the pilot with questions, "Well," he said, at last, "it was no use to argue. We tried it, In the half-hearted way that people do that don't mean it. Every one was his friend here on the Kanawha, and we knew It was the first time he ever had lost his bearings, but he knew, In such a thing as that, that the first and the last are the same time. When we had got through trying our worst to persuade him, he only Shook his head and says, 'I am done for, boys, and you know it,' Left the boat at Wheeling, and left his life on the river— Left his life on the earth, you may say, for I don't call it living, Setting there homesick at home for the wheel he can never go back to. Reads the river-news regular; knows just the stage of the water Up and down the whole way from Cincinnati to Pittsburg; Follows every boat from the time she starts out in the spring-time Till she lays up in the summer, and then again in the winter; Wants to talk all about her and who is her captain and pilot; Then wants to slide away to that everlastingly puzzling Thing that happened to him that morning on the Kanawha When he lost his bearings and North and South had changed places— No, I don't call that living, whatever the rest of you call it." We were silent again till that woman spoke up, "And what was it, Captain, that kept him from going back and being a pilot?" "Well, ma'am," after a moment the pilot patiently answered, "I don't hardly believe that I could explain it exactly."

He never, by any chance, quite kept his word, though there was a moment in every case when he seemed to imagine doing what he said, and he took with mute patience the rakings which the ladies gave him when he disappointed them.

Disappointed is not just the word, for the ladies did not really expect him to do what he said. They pretended to believe him when he promised, but at the bottom of their hearts they never did or could. He was gentle-mannered and soft-spoken, and when he set his head on one side, and said that a coat would be ready on Wednesday, or a dress on Saturday, and repeated his promise upon the same lady's expressed doubt, she would catch her breath and say that now she absolutely must have it on the day named, for otherwise she would not have a thing to put on. Then he would become very grave, and his soft tenor would deepen to a bass of unimpeachable veracity, and he would say, "Sure, lady, you have it."

The lady would depart still doubting and slightly sighing, and he would turn to the customer who was waiting to have a button sewed on, or something like that, and ask him softly what it was he could do for him. If the customer offered him his appreciation of the case in hand, he would let his head droop lower, and in a yet deeper bass deplore the doubt of the ladies as an idiosyncrasy of their sex. He would make the customer feel that he was a favorite customer whose rights to a perfect fidelity of word and deed must by no means be tampered with, and he would have the button sewed on or the rip sewed up at once, and refuse to charge anything, while the customer waited in his shirt-sleeves in the small, stuffy shop opening directly from the street. When he tolerantly discussed the peculiarities of ladies as a sex, he would endure to be laughed at, "for sufferance was the badge of all his tribe," and possibly he rather liked it.

The favorite customer enjoyed being there when some lady came back on the appointed Wednesday or Saturday, and the tailor came soothingly forward and showed her into the curtained alcove where she was to try on the garments, and then called into the inner shop for them. The shirt-sleeved journeyman, with his unbuttoned waistcoat-front all pins and threaded needles, would appear in his slippers with the things barely basted together, and the tailor would take them, with an airy courage, as if they were perfectly finished, and go in behind the curtain where the lady was waiting in a dishabille which the favorite customer, out of reverence for the sex, forbore to picture to himself. Then sounds of volcanic fury would issue from the alcove. "Now, Mr. Morrison, you have lied to me again, deliberately lied. Didn't I tell you I must have the things perfectly ready to-day? You see yourself that it will be another week before I can have my things."

"A week? Oh, madam! But I assure you—"

"Don't talk to me any more! It's the last time I shall ever come to you, but I suppose I can't take the work away from you as it is. When shall I have it?"

"To-morrow. Yes, to-morrow noon. Sure!"

"Now you know you are always out at noon. I should think you would be ashamed."

"If it hadn't been for sickness in the family I would have finished your dress with my own hands. Sure I would. If you come here to-morrow noon you find your dress all ready for you."

"I know I won't, but I will come, and you'd better have it ready."

"Oh, sure."

The lady then added some generalities of opprobrium with some particular criticisms of the garments. Her voice sank into dispassionate murmurs in these, but it rose again in her renewed sense of the wrong done her, and when she came from the alcove she went out of the street door purple. She reopened it to say, "Now, remember!" before she definitely disappeared.

"Rather a stormy session, Mr. Morrison," the customer said.

"Something fierce," Mr. Morrison sighed. But he did not seem much troubled, and he had one way with all his victims, no matter what mood they came or went in.

One day the customer was by when a kind creature timidly upbraided him. "This is the third time you've disappointed me, Mr. Morrison. I really wish you wouldn't promise me unless you mean to do it. I don't think it's right for you."

"Oh, but sure, madam! The things will be done, sure. We had a strike on us."

"Well, I will trust you once more," the kind creature said.

"You can depend on me, madam, sure."

When she was gone the customer said: "I wonder you do that sort of thing, Mr. Morrison. You can't be surprised at their behaving rustily with you if you never keep your word."

"Why, I assure you there are times when I don't know where to look, the way they go on. It is something awful. You ought to hear them once. And now they want the wote." He rearranged some pieces of tumbled goods at the table where the customer sat, and put together the disheveled leaves of the fashion-papers which looked as if the ladies had scattered them in their rage.

One day the customer heard two ladies waiting for their disappointments in the outer room while the tailor in the alcove was trying to persuade a third lady that positively her things would be sent home the next day before dark. The customer had now formed the habit of having his own clothes made by the tailor, and his system in avoiding disappointment was very simple. In the early fall he ordered a spring suit, and in the late spring it was ready. He never had any difficulty, but he was curious to learn how the ladies managed, and he listened with all his might while these two talked.

"I always wonder we keep coming," one of them said.

"I'll tell you why," the other said. "Because he's cheap, and we get things from a fourth to a third less than we can get them anywhere else. The quality is first rate, and he's absolutely honest. And, besides, he's a genius. The wretch has touch. The things have a style, a look, a hang! Really it's something wonderful. Sure it iss," she ended in the tailor's accent, and then they both laughed and joined in a common sigh.

"Well, I don't believe he means to deceive any one."

"Oh, neither do I. I believe he expects to do everything he says. And one can't help liking him even when he doesn't."

"He's a good while getting through with her," the first lady said, meaning the unseen lady in the alcove.

"She'll be a good while longer getting through with him, if he hasn't them ready the next time," the second lady said.

But the lady in the alcove issued from it with an impredicable smile, and the tailor came up to the others, and deferred to their wishes with a sort of voiceless respect.

He gave the customer a glance of good-fellowship, and said to him, radiantly: "Your things all ready for you, this morning. As soon as I—"

"Oh, no hurry," the customer responded.

"I won't be a minute," the tailor said, pulling the curtain of the alcove aside, and then there began those sounds of objurgation and expostulation, although the ladies had seemed so amiable before.

The customer wondered if they did not all enjoy it; the ladies in their patience under long trial, and the tailor in the pleasure of practising upon it. But perhaps he did believe in the things he promised. He might be so much a genius as to have no grasp of facts; he might have thought that he could actually do what he said.

The customer's question on these points found answer when one day the tailor remarked, as it were out of a clear sky, that he had sold his business; sold it to the slippered journeyman who used to come in his shirt-sleeves, with his vest-front full of pins and needles, bringing the basted garments to be tried on the ladies who had been promised them perfectly finished.

"He will do your clothes all right," he explained to the customer. "He is a first-rate cutter and fitter; he knows the whole business."

"But why—why—" the customer began.

"I couldn't stand it. The way them ladies would talk to a person, when you done your best to please them; it's something fierce."

"Yes, I know. But I thought you liked it, from the way you always promised them and never kept your word."

"And if I hadn't promised them?" the tailor returned with some show of feeling. "They wanted me to promise them—they made me—they wouldn't have gone away without it. Sure. Every one wanted her things before every one. You had got to think of that."

"But you had to think of what they would say."

"Say? Sometimes I thought they would hit me. One lady said she had a notion to slap me once. It's no way to talk."

"But you didn't seem to mind it."

"I didn't mind it for a good while. Then I couldn't stand it. So I sold."

He shook his head sadly; but the customer had no comfort to offer him. He asked when his clothes would be done, and the tailor told him when, and then they were not. The new proprietor tried them on, but he would not say just when they would be finished.

"We have a good deal of work already for some ladies that been disappointed. Now we try a new way. We tell people exactly what we do."

"Well, that's right," the customer said, but in his heart he was not sure he liked the new way.

The day before his clothes were promised he dropped in. From the curtained alcove he heard low murmurs, the voice of the new proprietor and the voice of some lady trying on, and being severely bidden not to expect her things at a time she suggested. "No, madam. We got too much work on hand already. These things, they will not be done before next week."

"I told you to-morrow," the same voice said to another lady, and the new proprietor came out with an unfinished coat in his hand.

"I know you did, but I thought you would be better than your word, and so I came to-day. Well, then, to-morrow."

"Yes, to-morrow," the new proprietor said, but he did not seem to have liked the lady's joke. He did not look happy.

A few weeks after that the customer came for some little alterations in his new suit.

In the curtained alcove he heard the murmurs of trying on, much cheerfuller murmurs than before; the voice of a lady lifted in gladness, in gaiety, and an incredible voice replying, "Oh, sure, madam."

Then the old proprietor came out in his shirt-sleeves and slippers, with his waistcoat-front full of pins and needles, just like the new proprietor in former days.

"Why!" the customer exclaimed. "Have you bought back?"

"No. I'm just here like a journeyman already. The new man he want me to come. He don't get along very well with his way. He's all right; he's a good man and a first-class tailor. But," and the former proprietor looked down at the basted garment hanging over his arm, and picked off an irrelevant thread from it, "he thinks I get along better with the ladies."

V
SOMEBODY'S MOTHER

The figure of a woman sat crouched forward on one of the lowermost steps of the brownstone dwelling which was keeping a domestic tradition in a street mostly gone to shops and small restaurants and local express-offices. The house was black behind its closed shutters, and the woman remained sitting there because no one could have come out of its door for a year past to hunt her away. The neighborhood policeman faltered in going by, and then he kept on. The three people who came out of the large, old-fashioned hotel, half a block off, on their way for dinner to a French table d'hôte which they had heard of, stopped and looked at the woman. They were a father and his son and daughter, and it was something like a family instinct that controlled them, in their pause before the woman crouching on the steps.

It was the early dusk of a December day, and the day was very chilly. "She seems to be sick or something," the father vaguely surmised. "Or asleep."

The three looked at the woman, but they did nothing for a moment. They would rather have gone on, but they waited to see if anything would happen to release them from the spell that they seemed to have laid upon themselves. They were conditional New-Yorkers of long sojourn, and it was from no apparent motive that the son wore evening dress, which his unbuttoned overcoat discovered, and an opera-hat. He would not have dressed so for that problematical French table d'hôte; probably he was going on later to some society affair. He now put in effect the father's impulse to go closer and look at the woman.

"She seems to be asleep," he reported.

"Shouldn't you think she would take cold? She will get her death there. Oughtn't we to do something?" the daughter asked, but she left it to the father, and he said:

"Probably somebody will come by."

"That we could leave her to?" the daughter pursued.

"We could do that without waiting," the son commented.

"Well, yes," the father assented; but they did not go on. They waited, helplessly, and then somebody came by. It was a young girl, not very definite in the dusk, except that she was unmistakably of the working class; she was simply dressed, though with the New York instinct for clothes. Their having stopped there seemed to stay her involuntarily, and after a glance in the direction of their gaze she asked the daughter:

"Is she sick, do you think?"

"We don't know what's the matter. But she oughtn't to stay there."

Something velvety in the girl's voice had made its racial quality sensible to the ear; as she went up to the crouching woman and bent forward over her and then turned to them, a street lamp threw its light on her face, and they saw that she was a light shade of colored girl.

"She seems to be sleeping."

"Perhaps," the son began, "she's not quite—" But he did not go on.

The girl looked round at the others and suggested, "She must be somebody's mother!"

The others all felt abashed in their several sorts and degrees, but in their several sorts and degrees they all decided that there was something romantic, sentimental, theatrical in the girl's words, like something out of some cheap story-paper story.

The father wondered if that kind of thing was current among that kind of people. He had a sort of esthetic pleasure in the character and condition expressed by the words.

"Well, yes," he said, "if she has children, or has had." The girl looked at him uncertainly, and then he added, "But, of course—"

The son went up to the woman again, and asked: "Aren't you well? Can we do anything for you? It won't do to stay here, you know." The woman only made a low murmur, and he said to his sister, "Suppose we get her up."

His sister did not come forward promptly, and the colored girl said, "I'll help you."

She took one arm of the woman and the son took the other, and they lifted her, without her connivance, to her feet and kept her on them. Then they walked her down the steps. On the level below she showed taller than either of them; she was bundled up in different incoherent wraps; her head was muffled, and she wore a battered bonnet at an involuntary slant.

"I don't know exactly what we shall do with her," the son said.

"We ought to get her home somehow," the daughter said.

The father proposed nothing, but the colored girl said, "If we keep walking her along, we'll come to a policeman and we can—"

A hoarse rumble of protest came from the muffled head of the woman, and the girl put her ear closer. "Want to go home? Well, the policeman will take you. We don't know where you live, and we haven't the time."

The woman seemed to have nothing to say further, and they began walking her westward; the colored girl supported her on one hand, and the son, in his evening dress and opera-hat, on the other.

The daughter followed in a vague anxiety, but the father went along, enjoying the anomaly, and happy in his relish of that phrase, "She must be somebody's mother." It now sounded to him like a catch from one of those New York songs, popular in the order of life where the mother represents what is best and holiest. He recalled a vaudeville ballad with the refrain of "A Boy's Best Friend is his Mother," which, when he heard it in a vaudeville theater, threatened the gallery floor under the applauding feet of the frenzied audience. Probably this colored girl belonged to that order of life; he wished he could know her social circumstance and what her outlook on the greater world might be. She seemed a kind creature, poor thing, and he respected her. "Somebody's mother"—he liked that.

They all walked westward, aimlessly, except that the table d'hôte where they had meant to dine was in that direction; they had heard of it as an amusingly harmless French place, and they were fond of such mild adventures.

The old woman contributed nothing to the definition of their progress. She stumbled and mumbled along, but between Seventh Avenue and Eighth she stubbornly arrested her guardians. "She says"—the colored girl translated some obscure avowal across her back—"she says she wants to go home, and she lives up in Harlem."

"Oh, well, that's good," the father said, with an optimistic amiability. "We'd better help walk her across to Ninth Avenue and put her on a car, and tell the conductor where to let her off."

He was not helping walk her himself, but he enjoyed his son's doing it in evening dress and opera-hat, with that kind colored girl on the other side of the mother; the composition was agreeably droll. The daughter did not like it, and she cherished the ideal of a passing policeman to take the old woman in charge.

No policeman passed, though great numbers of other people met them without apparently finding anything noticeable in the spectacle which their group presented. Among the crowds going and coming on the avenues which they crossed scarcely any turned to look at them, or was moved by the sense of anything odd in them.

The old woman herself did nothing to attract public notice till they were midway between Seventh and Eighth avenues. She mumbled something from time to time which the colored girl interpreted to the rest as her continued wish to go home. She was now clearer about her street and number. The girl, as if after question of her own generous spirit, said she did not see how she could go with her; she was expected at home herself.

"Oh, you won't have to go with her; we'll just put her aboard the Ninth Avenue car," the father encouraged her. He would have encouraged any one; he was enjoying the whole affair.

At a certain moment, for no apparent reason, the mother decided to sit down on a door-step. It proved to be the door-step of a house where from time to time colored people—sometimes of one sex, sometimes of another—went in or came out. The door seemed to open directly into a large room where dancing and dining were going on concurrently. At a long table colored people sat eating, and behind their chairs on both sides of the room and at the ends of the table colored couples were waltzing.

The effect was the more curious because, except for some almost inaudible music, the scene passed in silence. Those who were eating were not visibly incommoded by those revolving at their backs; the waltzers turned softly around and around, untempted by the table now before them, now behind them. When some of the diners or dancers came out, they stumbled over the old woman on the door-step without minding or stopping to inquire. Those outside, when they went in, fell over her with like equanimity and joined the strange company within.

The father murmured to himself the lines,

"'Vast forms that move fantastically
To a discordant melody—'"

with a remote trouble of mind because the words were at once so graphic and yet so imperfectly applicable. The son and daughter exchanged a silent wonder as long as they could bear it; then the daughter asked the colored girl:

"What is it?"

"It's a boarding-house," the girl answered, simply.

"Oh," the daughter said.

Sounds of more decided character than before now came from the figure on the door-step.

"She seems to be saying something," the daughter suggested in general terms. "What is she saying?" she asked the colored girl.

The girl stooped over and listened. Then she answered, "She's swearing."

"Swearing? What about? Whom is she swearing at?"

"At me, I reckon. She says, why don't I take her home."

"Well, why doesn't she get up, then?"

"She says she won't."

"We can't carry her to the car," the daughter noted.

"Oh, why not?" the father merrily demanded.

The daughter turned to her brother. They were both very respectful to their father, but the son agreed with his sister when she said: "Papa would joke about anything. But this has passed a joke. We must get this old thing up and start her off."

Upon experiment they could not get the old thing up, even with the help of the kind colored girl. They had to let her be, and the colored girl reported, after stooping over her again, "She says she can't walk."

"She walked here well enough," the daughter said.

"Not very well," the father amended.

His daughter did not notice him. She said to her brother: "Well, now you must go and find a policeman. It's strange none has gone by."

It was also strange that still their group remained without attracting the notice of the passers. Nobody stopped to speak or even stare; perhaps the phenomena of that boarding-house had ceased to have surprises for the public of the neighborhood, and they in their momentary relation to it would naturally be without interest.

The brother went away, leaving his sister with their father and that kind colored creature in charge of the old woman, now more and more quiescent on the door-step; she had ceased to swear, or even to speak. The brother came back after a time that seemed long, and said that he could not find a policeman anywhere, and at the same moment, as if the officer had been following at his heels, a policeman crossed the street from just behind him.

The daughter ran after him, and asked if he would not come and look at the old woman who had so steadfastly remained in their charge, and she rapidly explained.

"Sure, lady," the policeman said, and he turned from crossing the street and went up to the old woman. He laid his hand on her shoulder, and his touch seemed magical. "What's the matter? Can't you stand up?" She stood up as if at something familiar in the voice of authority. "Where do you live?" She gave an address altogether different from that she had given before—a place on the next avenue, within a block or two. "You'd better go home. You can walk, can't you?"

"I can walk well enough," she answered in a tone of vexation, and she made her word good by walking quite actively away in the direction she had given.

The kind colored girl became a part of the prevalent dark after refusing the thanks of the others. The daughter then fervently offered them to the policeman.

"That's all right, lady," he said, and the incident had closed except for her emotion at seeing him enter a police-station precisely across the street, where they could have got a dozen policemen in a moment.

"Well," the father said, "we might as well go to our French table d'hôte now."

"Oh," the son said, as if that reminded him, "the place seems to be shut."

"Well, then, we might as well go back to the hotel," the father decided. "I dare say we shall do quite as well there."

On the way the young people laughed over the affair and their escape from it, especially at the strange appearance and disappearance of the kind colored girl, with her tag of sentiment, and at the instant compliance of the old woman with the suggestion of the policeman.

The father followed, turning the matter over in his mind. Did mere motherhood hallow that old thing to the colored girl and her sort and condition? Was there a superstition of motherhood among such people which would endear this disreputable old thing to their affection and reverence? Did such people hold mothers in tenderer regard than people of larger means? Would a mother in distress or merely embarrassment instantly appeal to their better nature as a case of want or sickness in the neighborhood always appealed to their compassion? Would her family now welcome the old thing home from her aberration more fondly than the friends of one who had arrived in a carriage among them in a good street? But, after all, how little one knew of other people! How little one knew of one self, for that matter! How next to nothing one knew of Somebody's Mother! It did not necessarily follow from anything they knew of her that she was a mother at all. Her motherhood might be the mere figment of that kind colored girl's emotional fancy. She might be Nobody's Mother.

When it came to this the father laughed, too. Why, anyhow, were mothers more sacred than fathers? If they had found an old man in that old woman's condition on those steps, would that kind colored girl have appealed to them in his behalf as Somebody's Father?

VI
THE FACE AT THE WINDOW

He had gone down at Christmas, where our host

Had opened up his house on the Maine coast,
For the week's holidays, and we were all,
On Christmas night, sitting in the great hall,
About the corner fireplace, while we told
Stories like those that people, young and old,
Have told at Christmas firesides from the first,
Till one who crouched upon the hearth, and nursed
His knees in his claspt arms, threw back his head,
And fixed our host with laughing eyes, and said,
"This is so good, here—with your hickory logs
Blazing like natural-gas ones on the dogs,
And sending out their flicker on the wall
And rafters of your mock-baronial hall,
All in fumed-oak, and on your polished floor,
And the steel-studded panels of your door—
I think you owe the general make-believe
Some sort of story that will somehow give
A more ideal completeness to our case,
And make each several listener in his place—
Or hers—sit up, with a real goose-flesh creeping
All over him—or her—in proper keeping
With the locality and hour and mood.
Come!" And amid the cries of "Yes!" and "Good!"
Our host laughed back; then, with a serious air,
Looked around him on our hemicycle, where
He sat midway of it. "Why," he began,
But interrupted by the other man,
He paused for him to say: "Nothing remote,
But something with the actual Yankee note
Of here and now in it!" "I'll do my best,"
Our host replied, "to satisfy a guest.
What do you say to Barberry Cove? And would
Five years be too long past?" "No, both are good.
Go on!" "You noticed that big house to-day
Close to the water, and the sloop that lay,
Stripped for the winter, there, beside the pier?
Well, there she has lain just so, year after year;
And she will never leave her pier again;
But once, each spring she sailed in sun or rain,
For Bay Chaleur—or Bay Shaloor, as they
Like better to pronounce it down this way."

"I like Shaloor myself rather the best.
But go ahead," said the exacting guest.
And with a glance around at us that said,

"Don't let me bore you!" our host went ahead.

"Captain Gilroy built the big house, and he
Still lives there with his aging family.
He built the sloop, and when he used to come
Back from the Banks he made her more his home,
With his two boys, than the big house. The two
Counted with him a good half of her crew,
Until it happened, on the Banks, one day
The oldest boy got in a steamer's way,
And went down in his dory. In the fall
The others came without him. That was all
That showed in either one of them except
That now the father and the brother slept
Ashore, and not on board. When the spring came
They sailed for the old fishing-ground the same
As ever. Yet, not quite the same. The brother,
If you believed what folks say, kissed his mother
Good-by in going; and by general rumor,
The father, so far yielding as to humor
His daughters' weakness, rubbed his stubbly cheek
Against their lips. Neither of them would speak,
But the dumb passion of their love and grief
In so much show at parting found relief.

"The weeks passed and the months. Sometimes they heard
At home, by letter, from the sloop, or word
Of hearsay from the fleet. But by and by
Along about the middle of July,
A time in which they had no news began,
And holding unbrokenly through August, ran
Into September. Then, one afternoon,
While the world hung between the sun and moon,
And while the mother and her girls were sitting
Together with their sewing and their knitting,—
Before the early-coming evening's gloom
Had gathered round them in the living-room,
Helplessly wondering to each other when
They should hear something from their absent men,—
They saw, all three, against the window-pane,
A face that came and went, and came again,
Three times, as though for each of them, about
As high up from the porch's floor without

As a man's head would be that stooped to stare
Into the room on their own level there.
Its eyes dwelt on them wistfully as if
Longing to speak with the dumb lips some grief
They could not speak. The women did not start
Or scream, though each one of them, in her heart,
Knew she was looking on no living face,
But stared, as dumb as it did, in her place."

Here our host paused, and one sigh broke from all
Our circle whom his tale had held in thrall.
But he who had required it of him spoke
In what we others felt an ill-timed joke:
"Well, this is something like!" A girl said, "Don't!"
As if it hurt, and he said, "Well, I won't.
Go on!" And in a sort of muse our host
Said: "I suppose we all expect a ghost
Will sometimes come to us. But I doubt if we
Are moved by its coming as we thought to be.
At any rate, the women were not scared,
But, as I said, they simply sat and stared
Till the face vanished. Then the mother said,
'It was your father, girls, and he is dead.'
But both had known him; and now all went on
Much as before till three weeks more were gone,
When, one night sitting as they sat before,
Together with their mother, at the door
They heard a fumbling hand, and on the walk
Up from the pier, the tramp and muffled talk
Of different wind-blown voices that they knew
For the hoarse voices of their father's crew.
Then the door opened, and their father stood
Before them, palpably in flesh and blood.
The mother spoke for all, her own misgiving:
'Father, is this your ghost? Or are you living?'
'I am alive!' 'But in this very place
We saw your face look, like a spirit's face,
There through that window, just three weeks ago,
And now you are alive!' 'I did not know
That I had come; all I know is that then
I wanted to tell you folks here that our Ben
Was dying of typhoid fever. He raved of you
So that I could not think what else to do.
He's there in Bay Shaloor!'

"Well, that's the end."
And rising up to mend the fire our friend
Seemed trying to shun comment; but in vain:
The exacting guest came at him once again;
"You must be going to fall down, I thought,
There at the climax, when your story brought
The skipper home alive and well. But no,
You saved yourself with honor." The girl said, "Oh,"
Who spoke before, "it's wonderful! But you,
How could you think of anything so true,
So delicate, as the father's wistful face
Coming there at the window in the place
Of the dead son's! And then, that quaintest touch,
Of half-apology—that he felt so much,
He had to come! How perfectly New England! Well,
I hope nobody will undertake to tell
A common or garden ghost-story to-night."

Our host had turned again, and at her light
And playful sympathy he said, "My dear,
I hope that no one will imagine here
I have been inventing in the tale that's done.
My little story's charm if it has one
Is from no skill of mine. One does not change
The course of fable from its wonted range
To such effect as I have seemed to do:
Only the fact could make my story true."

VII
AN EXPERIENCE

For a long time after the event my mind dealt with the poor man in helpless conjecture, and it has now begun to do so again for no reason that I can assign. All that I ever heard about him was that he was some kind of insurance man. Whether life, fire, or marine insurance I never found out, and I am not sure that I tried to find out.

There was something in the event which discharged him of all obligation to define himself of this or that relation to life. He must have had some relation to it such as we all bear, and since the question of him has come up with me again I have tried him in several of those relations—father, son, brother, husband—without identifying him very satisfyingly in either.

As I say, he seemed by what happened to be liberated from the debt we owe in that kind to one another's curiosity, sympathy, or whatever. I cannot say what errand it was that brought him to the place, a strange, large, indeterminate open room, where several of us sat occupied with different sorts of business, but, as it seems to me now, by only a provisional right to the place. Certainly the corner allotted to my own editorial business was of temporary assignment; I was there until we could find a more permanent office. The man had nothing to do with me or with the publishers; he had no manuscript, or plan for an article which he wished to propose and to talk himself into writing, so that he might bring it with a claim to acceptance, as though he had been asked to write it. In fact, he did not even look of the writing sort; and his affair with some other occupant of that anomalous place could have been in no wise literary. Probably it was some kind of insurance business, and I have been left with the impression of fussiness in his conduct of it; he had to my involuntary attention an effect of conscious unwelcome with it.

After subjectively dealing with this impression, I ceased to notice him, without being able to give myself to my own work. The day was choking hot, of a damp that clung about one, and forbade one so much effort as was needed to relieve one of one's discomfort; to pull at one's wilted collar and loosen the linen about one's reeking neck meant exertion which one willingly forbore; it was less suffering to suffer passively than to suffer actively. The day was of the sort which begins with a brisk heat, and then, with a falling breeze, decays into mere swelter. To come indoors out of the sun was no escape from the heat; my window opened upon a shaded alley where the air was damper without being cooler than the air within.

At last I lost myself in my work with a kind of humid interest in the psychological inquiry of a contributor who was dealing with a matter rather beyond his power. I did not think that he was fortunate in having cast his inquiry in the form of a story; I did not think that his contrast of love and death as the supreme facts of life was what a subtler or stronger hand could have made it, or that the situation gained in effectiveness from having the hero die in the very moment of his acceptance. In his supposition that the reader would care more for his hero simply because he had undergone that tremendous catastrophe, the writer had omitted to make him interesting otherwise; perhaps he could not.

My mind began to wander from the story and not very relevantly to employ itself with the question of how far our experiences really affect our characters. I remembered having once classed certain temperaments as the stuff of tragedy, and others as the stuff of comedy, and of having found a greater cruelty in the sorrows which light natures undergo, as unfit and disproportionate for them. Disaster, I tacitly decided, was the fit lot of serious natures; when it befell the frivolous it was more than they ought to have been made to bear; it was not of their quality. Then by the mental zigzagging which all thinking is I thought of myself and whether I was of this make or that. If it was more creditable to be of serious stuff than frivolous, though I had no agency in choosing, I asked myself how I should be affected by the sight of certain things, like the common calamities reported every day in the papers which I had hitherto escaped seeing. By another zigzag I thought that I had never known a day so close and stifling and humid. I then reflected upon the comparative poverty of the French language, which I was told had only that one word for the condition we could call by half a dozen different names, as humid, moist, damp, sticky, reeking, sweltering, and so on. I supposed that a book of synonyms would give even more English adjectives; I thought of looking, but my book of synonyms was at the back of my table, and I would have to rise for it. Then I questioned whether the French language was so destitute of adjectives, after all; I preferred to doubt it rather than rise.

With no more logic than those other vagaries had, I realized that the person who had started me in them was no longer in the room. He must have gone outdoors, and I visualized him in the street pushing about, crowded hither and thither, and striking against other people as he went and came. I was glad I was not in his place; I believed I should have fallen in a faint from the heat, as I had once almost done in New York on a day like that. From this my mind jumped to the thought of sudden death in general. Was it such a happy thing as people pretended? For the person himself, yes, perhaps; but not for those whom he had left at home, say, in the morning, and who were expecting him at home in the evening. I granted that it was generally accepted as the happiest death, but no one that had tried it had said so. To be sure, one was spared a long sickness, with suffering from pain and from the fear of death. But one had no time for making one's peace with God, as it used to be said, and after all there might be something in death-bed repentance, although cultivated people no longer believed in it. Then I reverted to the family unprepared for the sudden death: the mother, the wife, the children. I struggled to get away from the question, but the vagaries which had lightly dispersed themselves before clung persistently to the theme now. I felt that it was like a bad dream. That was a promising diversion. Had one any sort of volition in the quick changes of dreams? One was aware of finding a certain nightmare insupportable, and of breaking from it as by main force, and then falling into a deep, sweet sleep. Was death something like waking from a dream such as that, which this life largely was, and then sinking into a long, restful slumber, and possibly never waking again?

Suddenly I perceived that the man had come back. He might have been there some time with his effect of fussing and his pathetic sense of unwelcome. I had not noticed; I only knew that he stood at the half-open door with the knob of it in his hand looking into the room blankly.

As he stood there he lifted his hand and rubbed it across his forehead as if in a sort of daze from the heat. I recognized the gesture as one very characteristic of myself; I had often rubbed my hand across my forehead on a close, hot day like that. Then the man suddenly vanished as if he had sunk through the floor.

People who had not noticed that he was there noticed now that he was not there. Some made a crooked rush toward the place where he had been, and one of those helpful fellow-men who are first in all needs lifted his head and mainly carried him into the wide space which the street stairs mounted to, and laid him on the floor. It was darker, if not cooler there, and we stood back to give him the air which he drew in with long, deep sighs. One of us ran down the stairs to the street for a doctor, wherever he might be found, and ran against a doctor at the last step.

The doctor came and knelt over the prostrate figure and felt its pulse, and put his ear down to its heart. It, which has already in my telling ceased to be he, drew its breath in those long suspirations which seemed to search each more profoundly than the last the lurking life, drawing it from the vital recesses and expelling it in those vast sighs.

They went on and on, and established in our consciousness the expectation of indefinite continuance. We knew that the figure there was without such consciousness as ours, unless it was something so remotely withdrawn that it could not manifest itself in any signal to our senses. There was nothing tragical in the affair, but it had a surpassing dignity. It was as if the figure was saying something to the life in each of us which none of us would have words to interpret, speaking some last message from the hither side of that bourne from which there is no returning.

There was a clutch upon my heart which tightened with the slower and slower succession of those awful breaths. Then one was drawn and expelled and then another was not drawn. I waited for the breathing to begin again, and it did not begin. The doctor rose from kneeling over the figure that had been a man, and uttered, with a kind of soundlessness, "Gone," and mechanically dusted his fingers with the thumbs of each hand from their contact with what had now become all dust forever.

That helpfulest one among us laid a cloth over the face, and the rest of us went away. It was finished. The man was done with the sorrow which, in our sad human order, must now begin for those he loved and who loved him. I tried vaguely to imagine their grief for not having been uselessly with him at the last, and I could not. The incident remained with me like an experience, something I had known rather than seen. I could not alienate it by my pity and make it another's. They whom it must bereave seemed for the time immeasurably removed from the fact.

VIII
THE BOARDERS

The boarder who had eloped was a student at the theological seminary, and he had really gone to visit his family, so that he had a fairly good conscience in giving this color to the fact that he was leaving the place permanently because he could not bear it any longer. It was a shade of deceit to connive with his room-mate for the custody of his carpet-bag and the few socks and collars and the one shirt and summer coat which did not visibly affect its lankness when gathered into it from his share of the bureau-drawers; but he did not know what else to do, and he trusted to a final forgiveness when all the facts were considered by a merciful providence. His board was fully paid, and he had suffered long. He argued with his room-mate that he could do no good by remaining, and that he would have stayed if he could have believed there was any use. Besides, the food was undermining his health, and the room with that broken window had given him a cold already. He had a right to go, and it was his duty to himself and the friends who were helping him through the seminary not to get sick.

He did not feel that he had convinced his room-mate, who took charge of his carpet-bag and now sat with it between his feet waiting the signal of the fugitive's surreptitious return for it. He was a vague-looking young man, presently in charge of the "Local and Literary" column of the one daily paper of the place, and he had just explained to the two other boarders who were watching with him for the event that he was not certain whether it was the supper, or the anxiety of the situation, or just what it was that was now affecting his digestion.

The fellow-boarders, who sat on the edge of the bed, in default of the one unbroken chair which their host kept for himself, as easier than a mattress to get up from suddenly, did not take sides for or against him in his theories of his discomfort. One of them glanced at the broken window.

"How do you glaze that in the daytime? You can't use the bolster then?"

"I'm not in, much, in the daytime."

It was a medical student who had spoken, but he was now silent, and the other said, after they had listened to the twitter of a piano in the parlor under the room, "That girl's playing will be the death of me."

"Not if her mother's cooking isn't," the medical student, whose name was Wallace, observed with a professional effect.

"Why don't you prescribe something for it?" the law student suggested.

"Which?" Wallace returned.

"I don't believe anything could cure the playing. I must have meant the cooking."

"You're a promising young jurist, Blakeley. What makes you think I could cure the cooking?"

"Oh, I just wondered. The sick one gets paler every day. I wonder what ails her."

"She's not my patient."

"Oh! Hippocratic oath. Rather fine of you, Wallace. But if she's not your patient—"

"Listen!" their host interrupted, sharply. After a joint silence he added: "No. It must have been the sleet."

"Well, Briggs," the law student said, "if it must have been the sleet, what mustn't it have been?"

"Oh!" Briggs explained, "I thought it was Phillips. He was to throw a handful of gravel at the window."

"And then you were to run down with his bag and help him to make his escape from a friendless widow. Well, I don't know that I blame him. If I didn't owe two weeks' board, I'd leave myself—though I hope I shouldn't sneak away. And if Mrs. Betterson didn't owe Wallace, here, two weeks' board, we'd walk off together arm-in-arm at high noon. I can't understand how he ever came to advance her the money."

Wallace rose from the bed, and kicked each leg out to dislodge the tight trousers of the middle eighteen-fifties which had caught on the tops of his high boots. "You're a tonguey fellow, Blakeley. But you'll find, as you live long, that there are several things you can't explain."

"I'll tell you what," Blakeley said. "We'll get Mrs. Betterson to take your loan for my debt, and we'll go at once."

"You can propose something like that before the justice of the peace in your first pettifogging case."

"I believe Wallace likes to stay. And yet he must know from his anatomical studies, better than the animals themselves, what cuts of meat the old lady gives us. I shouldn't be so fastidious about the cuts, if she didn't treat them all with pork gravy. Well, I mustn't be too hard on a lone widow that I owe board to. I don't suppose his diet had anything to do with the deep damnation of the late Betterson's taking off. Does that stove of yours smoke, Briggs?"

"Not when there isn't a fire in it."

"I just asked. Wallace's stove smokes, fire or no fire. It takes advantage of the old lady's indebtedness to him. There seem," he added, philosophically, "to be just two occupations open to widows who have to support themselves: millinery business for young ones, boarding-housing for old ones. It is rather restricted. What do you suppose she puts into the mince-pies? Mince-pies are rather a mystery at the best."

Wallace was walking up and down the room still in some difficulty with his trousers-legs, and kicking out from time to time to dislodge them. "How long should you say Blakeley had been going on?" he asked Briggs.

"You never can tell," Briggs responded. "I think he doesn't know himself."

"Well said, youthful scribe! With such listeners as you two, I could go on forever. Consider yourselves clapped jovially on the back, my gentle Briggs; I can't get up to do it from the hollow of your bed here. As you were saying, the wonder about these elderly widows who keep boarding-houses is the domestic dilapidation they fall into. If they've ever known how to cook a meal or sweep a room or make a bed, these arts desert them in the presence of their boarders. Their only aim in life seems to be preventing the escape of their victims, and they either let them get into debt for their board or borrow money from them. But why do they always have daughters, and just two of them: one beautiful, fashionable, and devoted to the piano; the other willing to work, but pale, pathetic, and incapable of the smallest achievement with the gridiron or the wash-board? It's a thing to make a person want to pay up and leave, even if he's reading law. If Wallace, here, had the spirit of a man, he would collect the money owing him, and—"

"Oh, stop it, Blakeley!" Wallace stormed. "I should think you'd get tired of your talk yourself."

"Well, as you insist—"

Blakeley began again, but Briggs jumped to his feet and caught up Phillips's carpet-bag, and looked wildly around. "It's gravel, this time."

"Well, take your hat, Briggs. It may be a prolonged struggle. But remember that Phillips's cause is just. He's paid his board, and he has a perfect right to leave. She has no right to prevent him. Think of that when the fray is at its worst. But try to get him off quietly, if you can. Deal gently with the erring, while you stand firm for boarders' rights. Remember that Phillips is sneaking off in order to spare her feelings and has come pretty near prevarication in the effort. Have you got your shoes off? No; it's your rubbers on. That's better."

Briggs faltered with the carpet-bag in his hand. "Boys, I don't like this. It feels—clandestine."

"It looks that way, too," Blakeley admitted. "It has an air of conspiracy."

"I've got half a mind to let Phillips come in and get his bag himself."

"It would serve him right, though I don't know why, exactly. He has a right to spare his own feelings if he's sparing hers at the same time. Of course he's afraid she'll plead with him to stay, and he'll have to be inexorable with her; and if I understand the yielding nature of Phillips he doesn't like to be inexorable."

There came another sharp rattle of small pebbles at the window.

"Oh, confound him!" Briggs cried under his breath, and he shuffled out of the room and crept noiselessly down the stairs to the front door. The door creaked a little in opening, and he left it ajar. The current of cold air that swept up to the companions he had left behind at his room door brought them the noise of his rush down the gravel walk to the gate and a noise there as of fugitive steps on the pavement outside.

A weak female tread made itself heard in the hallway, followed by a sharp voice from a door in the rear. "Was it the cat, Jenny?"

"No; the door just seems to have blown open. The catch is broken."

Swift, strong steps advanced with an effect of angry suspicion. "I don't believe it blew open. More likely the cat clawed it open."

The steps which the voice preceded seemed to halt at the open door, as if falling back from it, and Wallace and Blakeley, looking down, saw by the dim flare of the hall lamp the face of Briggs confronting the face of Mrs. Betterson from the outer darkness. They saw the sick girl, whose pallor they could not see, supporting herself by the stairs-post with one hand and pressing the other to her side.

"Oh! It's you, Mr. Briggs," the landlady said, with a note of inculpation. "What made you leave the door open?"

The spectators could not see the swift change in Briggs's face from terror to savage desperation, but they noted it in his voice. "Yes—yes! It's me. I just—I was just— No I won't, either! You'd better know the truth. I was taking Phillips's bag out to him. He was afraid to come in for it, because he didn't want to see you, the confounded coward! He's left."

"Left? And he said he would stay till spring! Didn't he, Jenny?"

"I don't remember—" the girl weakly gasped, but her mother did not heed her in her mounting wrath.

"A great preacher he'll make. What'd he say he left for?"

"He didn't say. Will you let me up-stairs?"

"No, I won't, till you tell me. You know well enough, between you."

"Yes, I do know," Briggs answered, savagely. "He left because he was tired of eating sole-leather for steak, and fire-salt pork, and tar for molasses, and butter strong enough to make your nose curl, and drinking burnt-rye slops for coffee and tea-grounds for tea. And so am I, and so are all of us, and—and— Will you let me go up-stairs now, Mrs. Betterson?"

His voice had risen, not so high but that another voice from the parlor could prevail over it: a false, silly, girl voice, with the twitter of piano-keys as from hands swept over the whole board to help drown the noise of the quarrel in the hall. "Oh yes, I'll sing it again, Mr. Saunders, if you sa-a-a-y."

Then this voice lifted itself in a silly song, and a silence followed the voices in the hall, except for the landlady's saying, brokenly: "Well, all right, Mr. Briggs. You can go up to your room for all me. I've tried to be a mother to you boys, but if this is what I get for it!"

The two at the threshold of Briggs's room retreated within, as he bounded furiously upon them and slammed the door after him. It started open again, from the chronic defect of the catch, but he did not care.

"Well, Briggs, I hope you feel better now," Blakeley began. "You certainly told her the truth, the whole truth, and nothing but the truth. But I wonder you had the heart to do it before that sick girl."

"I didn't have the heart," Briggs shouted. "But I had the courage, and if you say one word more, Blakeley, I'll throw you out of the room. I'm going to leave! My board's paid if yours isn't."

He went wildly about, catching things down here and there from nails and out of drawers. The tears stood in his eyes. But suddenly he stopped and listened to the sounds from below—the sound of the silly singing in the parlor, and the sound of sobbing in the dining-room, and the sound of vain entreating between the sobs.

"Oh, I don't suppose I'm fit to keep a boarding-house. I never was a good manager; and everybody imposes on me, and everything is so dear, and I don't know what's good from what's bad. Your poor father used to look after all that."

"Well, don't you cry, now, mother! It'll all come right, you'll see. I'm getting so I can go and do the marketing now; and if Minervy would only help a little—"

"No, no!" the mother's voice came anxiously up. "We can get along without her; we always have. I know he likes her, and I want to give her every chance. We can get along. If she was on'y married, once, we could all live—" A note of self-comforting gradually stole into the mother's voice, and the sound of a nose violently blown seemed to note a period in her suffering.

"Oh, mother, I wish I was well!" The girl's voice came with a burst of wild lamenting.

"'Sh, 'sh, deary!" her mother entreated. "He'll hear you, and then—"

"'Hazel Dell'?" the silly voice came from the parlor, with a sound of fright in it. "I can sing it without the music." The piano keys twittered the prelude and the voice sang:

"In the Hazel Dell my Nelly's sleeping,
Nelly loved so long!"

Wallace went forward and shut the door. "It's a shame to overhear them! What are you going to do, you fellows?"

"I'm going to stay," Briggs said, "if it kills me. At least I will till Minervy's married. I don't care what the grub's like. I can always get a bite at the restaurant."

"If anybody will pay up my back board, I'll stay, too," Blakeley followed. "I should like to make a virtue of it, and, as things stand, I can't."

"All right," Wallace said, and he went out and down the stairs. Then from the dining-room below his heavy voice offering encouragement came up, in terms which the others could not make out.

"I'll bet he's making her another advance," Blakeley whispered, as if he might be overheard by Wallace.

"I wish I could have made to do it," Briggs whispered back. "I feel as mean as pursley. Would you like to kick me?"

"I don't see how that would do any good. I may want to borrow money of you, and you can't ask a loan from a man you've kicked. Besides, I think what you said may do her good."

IX
BREAKFAST IS MY BEST MEAL
I

Breakfast is my best meal, and I reckon it's always been
Ever since I was old enough to know what breakfast could mean.
I mind when we lived in the cabin out on the Illinoy,
Where father had took up a quarter-section when I was a boy,
I used to go for the cows as soon as it was light;
And when I started back home, before I come in sight,
I come in smell of the cabin, where mother was frying the ham,
And boiling the coffee, that reached through the air like a mile o' ba'm,
'N' I bet you I didn't wait to see what it was that the dog
Thought he'd got under the stump or inside o' the hollow log!
But I made the old cows canter till their hoof-joints cracked—you know
That dry, funny kind of a noise that the cows make when they go—
And I never stopped to wash when I got to the cabin door;
I pulled up my chair and e't like I never had e't before.
And mother she set there and watched me eat, and eat, and eat,
Like as if she couldn't give her old eyes enough of the treat;
And she split the shortened biscuit, and spread the butter between,
And let it lay there and melt, and soak and soak itself in;
And she piled up my plate with potato and ham and eggs,
Till I couldn't hold any more, or hardly stand on my legs;
And she filled me up with coffee that would float an iron wedge,
And never give way a mite, or spill a drop at the edge.

II

What? Well, yes, this is good coffee, too. If they don't know much,
They do know how to make coffee, I will say that for these Dutch.
But my—oh, my! It ain't the kind of coffee my mother made,
And the coffee my wife used to make would throw it clear in the shade;
And the brand of sugar-cured, canvased ham that she always used—
Well, this Westphalia stuff would simply have made her amused!
That so, heigh? I saw that you was United States as soon
As ever I heard you talk; I reckon I know the tune!
Pick it out anywhere; and you understand how I feel
About these here foreign breakfasts: breakfast is my best meal.

III

My! but my wife was a cook; and the breakfasts she used to get
The first years we was married, I can smell 'em and taste 'em yet:
Corn cake light as a feather, and buckwheat thin as lace
And crisp as cracklin'; and steak that you couldn't have the face
To compare any steak over here to; and chicken fried
Maryland style—I couldn't get through the bill if I tried.
And then, her waffles! My! She'd kind of slip in a few
Between the ham and the chicken—you know how women'll do—
For a sort of little surprise, and, if I was running light,
To take my fancy and give an edge to my appetite.
Done it all herself as long as we was poor, and I tell you
She liked to see me eat as well as mother used to do;
I reckon she went ahead of mother some, if the truth was known,
And everything she touched she give a taste of her own.

IV

She was a cook, I can tell you! And after we got ahead,
And she could 'a' had a girl to do the cookin' instead,
I had the greatest time to get Momma to leave the work;
She said it made her feel like a mis'able sneak and shirk.
She didn't want daughter, though, when we did begin to keep girls,
To come in the kitchen and cook, and smell up her clo'es and curls;
But you couldn't have stopped the child, whatever you tried to do—
I reckon the gift of the cookin' was born in Girly, too.
Cook she would from the first, and we just had to let her alone;
And after she got married, and had a house of her own,
She tried to make me feel, when I come to live with her,
Like it was my house, too; and I tell you she done it, sir!
She remembered that breakfast was my best meal, and she tried
To have all I used to have, and a good deal more beside;
Grape-fruit to begin with, or melons or peaches, at least—
Husband's business took him there, and they had went to live East—
Then a Spanish macker'l, or a soft-shell crab on toast,
Or a broiled live lobster! Well, sir, I don't want to seem to boast,
But I don't believe you could have got in the whole of New York
Any such an oyster fry or sausage of country pork.

V

Well, I don't know what-all it means; I always lived just so—
Never drinked or smoked, and yet, here about two years ago,

I begun to run down; I ain't as young as I used to be;
And the doctors all said Carlsbad, and I reckon this is me.
But it's more like some one I've dreamt of, with all three of 'em gone!
Believe in ghosts? Well, I do. I know there are ghosts. I'm one.
Maybe I mayn't look it—I was always inclined to fat;
The doctors say that's the trouble, and very likely it's that.
This is my little grandson, and this is the oldest one
Of Girly's girls; and for all that the whole of us said and done,
She must come with grandpa when the doctors sent me off here,
To see that they didn't starve him. Ain't that about so, my dear?
She can cook, I tell you; and when we get home again
We're goin' to have something to eat; I'm just a-livin' till then.
But when I set here of a morning, and think of them that's gone—
Mother and Momma and Girly—well, I wouldn't like to let on
Before the children, but I can almost seem to see
All of 'em lookin' down, like as if they pitied me,
After the breakfasts they give me, to have me have to put up
With nothing but bread and butter, and a little mis'able cup
Of this here weak-kneed coffee! I can't tell how you feel,
But it fairly makes me sick! Breakfast is my best meal.

THE MOTHER-BIRD

She wore around the turned-up brim of her bolero-like toque a band of violets not so much in keeping with the gray of the austere November day as with the blue of her faded autumnal eyes. Her eyes were autumnal, but it was not from this, or from the lines of maturity graven on the passing prettiness of her little face, that the notion and the name of Mother-Bird suggested itself. She became known as the Mother-Bird to the tender ironic fancy of the earliest, if not the latest, of her friends, because she was slight and small, and like a bird in her eager movements, and because she spoke so instantly and so constantly of her children in Dresden: before you knew anything else of her you knew that she was going out to them.

She was quite alone, and she gave the sense of claiming their protection, and sheltering herself in the fact of them. When she mentioned her daughters she had the effect of feeling herself chaperoned by them. You could not go behind them and find her wanting in the social guarantees which women on steamers, if not men, exact of lonely birds of passage who are not mother-birds. One must respect the convention by which she safeguarded herself and tried to make good her standing; yet it did not lastingly avail her with other birds of passage, so far as they were themselves mother-birds, or sometimes only maiden-birds. The day had not ended before they began to hold her off by slight liftings of their wings and rufflings of their feathers, by quick, evasive flutterings, by subtle ignorances of her approach, which convinced no one but themselves that they had not seen her. She sailed with the sort of acquaintance-in-common which every one shares on a ship leaving port, when people are confused by the kindness of friends coming to see them off after sending baskets of fruit and sheaves of flowers, and scarcely know what they are doing or saying. But when the ship was abreast of Fire Island, and the pilot had gone over the side, these provisional intimacies of the parting hour began to restrict themselves. Then the Mother-Bird did not know half the women she had known at the pier, or quite all the men.

It was not that she did anything obvious to forfeit this knowledge. Her behavior was if anything too exemplary; it might be thought to form a reproach to others. Perhaps it was the unseasonable band of violets around her hat-brim; perhaps it was the vernal gaiety of her dress; perhaps it was the uncertainty of her anxious eyes, which presumed while they implored. A mother-bird must not hover too confidently, too appealingly, near coveys whose preoccupations she does not share. It might have been her looking and dressing younger than nature justified; at forty one must not look thirty; in November one must not, even involuntarily, wear the things of May if one would have others believe in one's devotion to one's children in Dresden; one alleges in vain one's impatience to join them as grounds for joining groups or detached persons who have begun to write home to their children in New York or Boston.

The very readiness of the Mother-Bird to give security by the mention of well-known names, to offer proof of her social solvency by the eager correctness of her behavior, created reluctance around her. Some would not have her at all from the first; others, who had partially or conditionally accepted her, returned her upon her hands and withdrew from the negotiation. More and more she found herself outside that hard woman-world, and trying less and less to beat her way into it.

The women may have known her better even than she knew herself, and it may have been through ignorance greater than her own that the men were more acquiescent. But the men too were not so acquiescent, or not at all, as time passed.

It would be hard to fix the day, the hour, far harder the moment, when the Mother-Bird began to disappear from the drawing-room and to appear in the smoking-room, or say whether she passed from the one to the other in a voluntary exile or by the rigor of the women's unwritten law. Still, from time to time she was seen in their part of the ship, after she was also seen where the band of violets showed strange and sad through veils of smoke that were not dense enough to hide her poor, pretty little face, with its faded blue eyes and wistful mouth. There she passed by quick transition from the conversation of the graver elderly smokers to the loud laughter of two birds of prey who became her comrades, or such friends as birds like them can be to birds like her.

From anything she had said or done there was no reason for her lapse from the women and the better men to such men; for her transition from the better sort of women there was no reason except that it happened. Whether she attached herself to the birds of prey, or they to her, by that instinct which enables birds of all kinds to know themselves of a feather remained a touching question.

There remained to the end the question whether she was of a feather with them, or whether it was by some mischance, or by some such stress of the elements as drives birds of any feather to flock with birds of any other. To the end there remained a distracted and forsaken innocence in her looks. It was imaginable that she had made overtures to the birds of prey because she had made overtures to every one else; she was always seeking rather than sought, and her acceptance with them was as deplorable as her refusal by better birds. Often they were seen without her, when they had that look of having escaped, which others wore; but she was not often seen without them.

There is not much walking-weather on a November passage, and she was seen less with them in the early dark outdoors than in the late light within, by which she wavered a small form through the haze of their cigars in the smoking-room, or in the grill-room, where she showed in faint eclipse through the fumes of the broiling and frying, or through the vapors of the hot whiskies. The birds of prey were then heard laughing, but whether at her or with her it must have been equally sorrowful to learn.

Perhaps they were laughing at the maternal fondness which she had used for introduction to the general acquaintance lost almost in the moment of winning it. She seemed not to resent their laughter, though she seemed not to join in it. The worst of her was the company she kept; but since no better would allow her to keep it, you could not confidently say she would not have liked the best company on board. At the same time you could not have said she would; you could not have been sure it would not have bored her. Doubtless these results are not solely the sport of chance; they must be somewhat the event of choice if not of desert.

For anything you could have sworn, the Mother-Bird would have liked to be as good as the best. But since it was not possible for her to be good in the society of the best, she could only be good in that of the worst. It was to be hoped that the birds of prey were not cruel to her; that their mockery was never unkind if ever it was mockery. The cruelty which must come came when they began to be seen less and less with her, even at the late suppers, through the haze of their cigars and the smoke of the broiling and frying, and the vapors of the hot whiskies. Then it was the sharpest pang of all to meet her wandering up and down the ship's promenades, or leaning on the rail and looking dimly out over the foam-whitened black sea. It is the necessity of birds of prey to get rid of other birds when they are tired of them, and it had doubtless come to that.

One night, the night before getting into port, when the curiosity which always followed her with grief failed of her in the heightened hilarity of the smoking-room, where the last bets on the ship's run were making, it found her alone beside a little iron table, of those set in certain nooks outside the grill-room. There she sat with no one near, where the light from within fell palely upon her. The boon birds of prey, with whom she had been supping, had abandoned her, and she was supporting her cheek on the small hand of the arm that rested on the table. She leaned forward, and swayed with the swaying ship; the violets in her bolero-toque quivered with the vibrations of the machinery. She was asleep, poor Mother-Bird, and it would have been impossible not to wish her dreams were kind.

XI
THE AMIGO

His name was really Perez Armando Aldeano, but in the end everybody called him the amigo, because that was the endearing term by which he saluted all the world. There was a time when the children called him "Span-yard" in their games, for he spoke no tongue but Spanish, and though he came from Ecuador, and was no more a Spaniard than they were English, he answered to the call of "Span-yard!" whenever he heard it. He came eagerly in the hope of fun, and all the more eagerly if there was a hope of mischief in the fun. Still, to discerning spirits, he was always the amigo, for, when he hailed you so, you could not help hailing him so again, and whatever mock he put upon you afterward, you were his secret and inalienable friend.

The moment of my own acceptance in this quality came in the first hours of expansion following our getting to sea after long detention in the dock by fog. A small figure came flying down the dock with outspread arms, and a joyful cry of "Ah, amigo!" as if we were now meeting unexpectedly after a former intimacy in Bogotá; and the amigo clasped me round the middle to his bosom, or more strictly speaking, his brow, which he plunged into my waistcoat. He was clad in a long black overcoat, and a boy's knee-pants, and under the peak of his cap twinkled the merriest black eyes that ever lighted up a smiling face of olive hue. Thereafter, he was more and more, with the thinness of his small black legs, and his habit of hopping up and down, and dancing threateningly about, with mischief latent in every motion, like a crow which in being tamed has acquired one of the worst traits of civilization. He began babbling and gurgling in Spanish, and took my hand for a stroll about the ship, and from that time we were, with certain crises of disaffection, firm allies.

There were others whom he hailed and adopted his friends, whose legs he clung about and impeded in their walks, or whom he required to toss him into the air as they passed, but I flattered myself that he had a peculiar, because a primary, esteem for myself. I have thought it might be that, Bogotá being said to be a very literary capital, as those things go in South America, he was mystically aware of a common ground between us, wider and deeper than that of his other friendships. But it may have been somewhat owing to my inviting him to my cabin to choose such portion as he would of a lady-cake sent us on shipboard at the last hour. He prattled and chuckled over it in the soft gutturals of his parrot-like Spanish, and rushed up on deck to eat the frosting off in the presence of his small companions, and to exult before them in the exploitation of a novel pleasure. Yet it could not have been the lady-cake which lastingly endeared me to him, for by the next day he had learned prudence and refused it without withdrawing his amity.

This, indeed, was always tempered by what seemed a constitutional irony, and he did not impart it to any one without some time making his friend feel the edge of his practical humor. It was not long before the children whom he gathered to his heart had each and all suffered some fall or bump or bruise which, if not of his intention, was of his infliction, and which was regretted with such winning archness that the very mothers of them could not resist him, and his victims dried their tears to follow him with glad cries of "Span-yard, Span-yard!" Injury at his hands was a favor; neglect was the only real grievance. He went about rolling his small black head, and darting roguish lightnings from under his thick-fringed eyes, and making more trouble with a more enticing gaiety than all the other people on the ship put together.

The truth must be owned that the time came, long before the end of the voyage, when it was felt that in the interest of the common welfare, something must be done about the amigo. At the conversational end of the doctor's table, where he was discussed whenever the racks were not on, and the talk might have languished without their inspiration, his badness was debated at every meal. Some declared him the worst boy in the world, and held against his half-hearted defenders that something ought to be done about him; and one was left to imagine all the darker fate for him because there was nothing specific in these convictions. He could not be thrown overboard, and if he had been put in irons probably his worst enemies at the conversational end of the table would have been the first to intercede for him. It is not certain, however, that their prayers would have been effective with the captain, if that officer, framed for comfort as well as command, could have known how accurately the amigo had dramatized his personal presence by throwing himself back, and clasping his hands a foot in front of his small stomach, and making a few tilting paces forward.

The amigo had a mimic gift which he liked to exercise when he could find no intelligible language for the expression of his ironic spirit. Being forbidden visits in and out of season to certain staterooms whose inmates feigned a wish to sleep, he represented in what grotesque attitudes of sonorous slumber they passed their day, and he spared neither age nor sex in these graphic shows. When age refused one day to go up on deck with him and pleaded in such Spanish as it could pluck up from its past studies that it was too old, he laughed it to scorn. "You are not old," he said. "Why?" the flattered dotard inquired. "Because you smile," and that seemed reason enough for one's continued youth. It was then that the amigo gave his own age, carefully telling the Spanish numerals over, and explaining further by holding up both hands with one finger shut in. But he had the subtlety of centuries in his nine years, and he penetrated the ship everywhere with his arch spirit of mischief. It was mischief always in the interest of the good-fellowship which he offered impartially to old and young; and if it were mere frolic, with no ulterior object, he did not care at all how old or young his playmate was. This endeared him naturally to every age; and the little blond German-American boy dried his tears from the last accident inflicted on him by the amigo to recall him by tender entreaties of "Span-yard, Span-yard!" while the eldest of his friends could not hold out against him more than two days in the strained relations following upon the amigo's sweeping him down the back with a toy broom employed by the German-American boy to scrub the scuppers. This was not so much an injury as an indignity, but it was resented as an indignity, in spite of many demure glances of propitiation from the amigo's ironical eyes and murmurs of inarticulate apology as he passed.

He was, up to a certain point, the kindest and truest of amigos; then his weird seizure came, and the baby was spilled out of the carriage he had been so benevolently pushing up and down; or the second officer's legs, as he walked past with the prettiest girl on board, were hit with the stick that the amigo had been innocently playing shuffle-board with; or some passenger was taken unawares in his vanity or infirmity and made to contribute to the amigo's passion for active amusement.

At this point I ought to explain that the amigo was not traveling alone from Ecuador to Paris, where it was said he was to rejoin his father. At meal-times, and at other rare intervals, he was seen to be in the charge of a very dark and very silent little man, with intensely black eyes and mustache, clad in raven hues from his head to the delicate feet on which he wore patent-leather shoes. With him the amigo walked gravely up and down the deck, and behaved decorously at table; and we could not reconcile the apparent affection between the two with a theory we had that the amigo had been found impossible in his own country, and had been sent out of Ecuador by a decree of the government, or perhaps a vote of the whole people. The little, dark, silent man, in his patent-leather boots, had not the air of conveying a state prisoner into exile, and we wondered in vain what the tie between him and the amigo was. He might have been his tutor, or his uncle. He exercised a quite mystical control over the amigo, who was exactly obedient to him in everything, and would not look aside at you when in his keeping. We reflected with awe and pathos that, as they roomed together, it was his privilege to see the amigo asleep, when that little, very kissable black head rested innocently on the pillow, and the busy brain within it was at peace with the world which formed its pleasure and its prey in waking.

It would be idle to represent that the amigo played his pranks upon that shipload of long-suffering people with final impunity. The time came when they not only said something must be done, but actually did something. It was by the hand of one of the amigo's sweetest and kindest friends, namely, that elderly captain, off duty, who was going out to be assigned his ship in Hamburg. From the first he had shown the affectionate tenderness for the amigo which was felt by all except some obdurate hearts at the conversational end of the table; and it must have been with a loving interest in the amigo's ultimate well-being that, taking him in an ecstasy of mischief, he drew the amigo face downward across his knees, and bestowed the chastisement which was morally a caress. He dismissed him with a smile in which the amigo read the good understanding that existed unimpaired between them, and accepted his correction with the same affection as that which had given it. He shook himself and ran off with an enjoyment of the joke as great as that of any of the spectators and far more generous.

In fact there was nothing mean in the amigo. Impish he was, or might be, but only in the sort of the crow or the parrot; there was no malevolence in his fine malice. One fancied him in his adolescence taking part in one of the frequent revolutions of his continent, but humorously, not homicidally. He would like to alarm the other faction, and perhaps drive it from power, or overset it from its official place, but if he had the say there would be no bringing the vanquished out into the plaza to be shot. He may now have been on his way to France ultimately to study medicine, which seems to be preliminary to a high political career in South America; but in the mean time we feared for him in that republic of severely regulated subordinations.

We thought with pathos of our early parting with him, as we approached Plymouth and tried to be kodaked with him, considering it an honor and pleasure. He so far shared our feeling as to consent, but he insisted on wearing a pair of glasses which had large eyes painted on them, and on being taken in the act of inflating a toy balloon. Probably, therefore, the likeness would not be recognized in Bogotá, but it will always be endeared to us by the memory of the many mockeries suffered from him. There were other friends whom we left on the ship, notably those of the conversational end of the table, who thought him simply a bad boy; but there were none of such peculiar appeal as he, when he stood by the guard, opening and shutting his hand in ironical adieu, and looking smaller and smaller as our tender drifted away and the vast liner loomed immense before us. He may have contributed to its effect of immensity by the smallness of his presence, or it may have dwarfed him. No matter; he filled no slight space in our lives while he lasted. Now that he is no longer there, was he really a bad little boy, merely and simply? Heaven knows, which alone knows good boys from bad.

XII
BLACK CROSS FARM
(To F. S.)

After full many a mutual delay
My friend and I at last fixed on a day
For seeing Black Cross Farm, which he had long
Boasted the fittest theme for tale or song
In all that charming region round about:
Something that must not really be left out
Of the account of things to do for me.
It was a teasing bit of mystery,
He said, which he and his had tried in vain,
Ever since they had found it, to explain.
The right way was to happen, as they did,
Upon it in the hills where it was hid;
But chance could not be always trusted, quite,
You might not happen on it, though you might;
Encores were usually objected to
By chance. The next best thing that we could do
Was in his carryall, to start together,
And trust that somehow favoring wind and weather,
With the eccentric progress of his horse,
Would so far drift us from our settled course
That we at least could lose ourselves, if not
Find the mysterious object that we sought.
So one blithe morning of the ripe July
We fared, by easy stages, toward the sky
That rested one rim of its turquoise cup
Low on the distant sea, and, tilted up,
The other on the irregular hilltops. Sweet
The sun and wind that joined to cool and heat
The air to one delicious temperature;
And over the smooth-cropt mowing-pieces pure

The pine-breath, borrowing their spicy scent
In barter for the balsam that it lent!
And when my friend handed the reins to me,
And drew a fuming match along his knee,
And, lighting his cigar, began to talk,
I let the old horse lapse into a walk
From his perfunctory trot, content to listen,
Amid that leafy rustle and that glisten
Of field, and wood, and ocean, rapt afar,
From every trouble of our anxious star.
From time to time, between effect and cause
In this or that, making a questioning pause,
My friend peered round him while he feigned a gay
Hope that we might have taken the wrong way
At the last turn, and then let me push on,
Or the old horse rather, slanting hither and yon,
And never in the middle of the track,
Except when slanting off or slanting back.
He talked, I listened, while we wandered by
The scanty fields of wheat and oats and rye,
With patches of potatoes and of corn,
And now and then a garden spot forlorn,
Run wild where once a house had stood, or where
An empty house yet stood, and seemed to stare
Upon us blindly from the twisted glass
Of windows that once let no wayfarer pass
Unseen of children dancing at the pane,
And vanishing to reappear again,
Pulling their mother with them to the sight.
Still we kept on, with turnings left and right,
Past farmsteads grouped in cheerful neighborhoods,
Or solitary; then through shadowy woods
Of pine or birch, until the road, grass-grown,
Had given back to Nature all her own
Save a faint wheel-trace, that along the slope,
Rain-gullied, seemed to stop and doubt and grope,
And then quite ceased, as if 't had turned and fled
Out of the forest into which it led,
And left us at the gate whose every bar
Was nailed against us. But, "Oh, here we are!"
My friend cried joyously. "At last, at last!"
And making our horse superfluously fast,
He led the way onward by what had been
A lane, now hid by weeds and briers between

Meadows scarce worth the mowing, to a space
Shaped as by Nature for the dwelling-place
Of kindly human life: a small plateau
Open to the heaven that seemed bending low
In liking for it. There beneath a roof
Still against winter and summer weather-proof,
With walls and doors and windows perfect yet,
Between its garden and its graveyard set,
Stood the old homestead, out of which had perished
The home whose memory it dumbly cherished,
And which, when at our push the door swung wide,
We might have well imagined to have died
And had its funeral the day before:
So clean and cold it was from floor to floor,
So lifelike and so deathlike, with the thrill
Of hours when life and death encountered still
Passionate in it. They that lay below
The tangled grasses or the drifted snow,
Husband and wife, mother and little one,
From that sad house less utterly were gone
Than they that living had abandoned it.
In moonless nights their Absences might flit,
Homesick, from room to room, or dimly sit
Around its fireless hearths, or haunt the rose
And lily in the neglected garden close;
But they whose feet had borne them from the door
Would pass the footworn threshold nevermore.
We read the moss-grown names upon the tombs,
With lighter melancholy than the glooms
Of the dead house shadowed us with, and thence
Turning, my heart was pierced with more intense
Suggestion of a mystical dismay,
As in the brilliance of the summer day
We faced the vast gray barn. The house was old,
Though so well kept, as age by years is told
In our young land; but the barn, gray and vast,
Stood new and straight and strong—all battened fast
At every opening; and where once the mow
Had yawned wide-windowed, on the sheathing now
A Cross was nailed, the bigness of a man,
Aslant from left to right, athwart the span,
And painted black as paint could make it. Hushed,
I stood, while manifold conjecture rushed
To this point and to that point, and then burst

In the impotent questionings rejected first.
What did it mean? Ah, that no one could tell.
Who put it there? That was unknown as well.
Was there no legend? My friend knew of none.
No neighborhood story? He had sought for one
In vain. Did he imagine it accident,
With nothing really implied or meant
By the boards set in that way? It might be,
But I could answer that as well as he.
Then (desperately) what did he guess it was:
Something of purpose, or without a cause
Other than chance? He slowly shook his head,
And with his gaze fixed on the symbol said:
"We have quite ceased from guessing or surmising,
For all our several and joint devising
Has left us finally where I must leave you.
But now I think it is your part to do
Yourself some guessing. I hoped you might bring
A fresh mind to the riddle's unraveling.
Come!"

And thus challenged I could not deny
The sort of right he had to have me try;
And yielding, I began—instinctively
Proceeding by exclusion: "We agree
It was not put there as a pious charm
To keep the abandoned property from harm?
The owner could have been no Catholic;
And yet it was no sacrilegious trick
To make folks wonder; and it was not chance
Assuredly that set those boards askance
In that shape, or before or after, so
Painted them to that coloring of woe.
Do you suppose, then, that it could have been
Some secret sorrow or some secret sin,
That tried to utter or to expiate
Itself in that way: some unhappy hate
Turned to remorse, or some life-rending grief
That could not find in years or tears relief?
Who lived here last?"

"Ah," my friend made reply,
"You know as much concerning that as I.
All I could tell is what those gravestones tell,
And they have told it all to you as well.

The names, the dates, the curious epitaphs
At whose quaint phrase one either sighs or laughs,
Just as one's heart or head happens to be
Hollow or not, are there for each to see.
But I believe they have nothing to reveal:
No wrong to publish, no shame to conceal."

"And yet that Cross!" I turned at his reply,
Fixing the silent symbol with my eye,
Insistently. "And you consent," I said,
"To leave the enigma uninterpreted?"

"Why, no," he faltered, then went on: "Suppose
That some one that had known the average woes
Of human nature, finding that the load
Was overheavy for him on life's road,
Had wished to leave some token in this Cross,
Of what had been his gain and been his loss,
Of what had been his suffering and of what
Had also been the solace of his lot?
Whoever that unknown brother-man might be,
I think he must have been like you and me,
Who bear our Cross, and when we fail at length,
Bow down and pray to it for greater strength."

I mused, and as I mused, I seemed to find
The fancy more and still more to my mind.

"Well, let it go at that! I think, for me,
I like that better than some tragedy
Of clearer physiognomy, which were
In being more definite the vulgarer.
For us, what, after all, would be the gain
Of making the elusive meaning plain?
I really think, if I were you and yours,
I would not lift the veil that now obscures
The appealing fact, lest I should spoil the charm
Deeding me for my own the Black Cross Farm."

"A good suggestion! I am glad," said he,
"We have always practised your philosophy."

He smiled, we laughed; we sighed and turned away,
And left the mystery to the summer day
That made as if it understood, and could
Have read the riddle to us if it would:

The wide, wise sky, the clouds that on the grass
Let their vague shadows dreamlike trail and pass;
The conscious woods, the stony meadows growing
Up to birch pastures, where we heard the lowing
Of one disconsolate cow. All the warm afternoon,
Lulled in a reverie by the myriad tune
Of insects, and the chirp of songless birds,
Forgetful of the spring-time's lyric words,
Drowsed round us while we tried to find the lane
That to our coming feet had been so plain,
And lost ourselves among the sweetfern's growth,
And thickets of young pine-trees, nothing loath,
Amidst the wilding loveliness to stray,
And spend, if need were, looking for the way,
Whole hours; but blundered into the right course
Suddenly, and came out upon our horse,
Where we had left him—to our great surprise,
Stamping and switching at the pestering flies,
But not apparently anxious to depart,
When nearly overturning at the start,
We followed down that evanescent trace
Which, followed up, had brought us to the place.

Then, all the wayside scenes reversing, we
Dropped to the glimpses of the distant sea,
Content as if we brought, returning thus,
The secret of the Black Cross back with us.

XIII
THE CRITICAL BOOKSTORE

It had long been the notion of Frederick Erlcort, who held it playfully, held it seriously, according to the company he was in, that there might be a censorship of taste and conscience in literary matters strictly affiliated with the retail commerce in books. When he first began to propose it, playfully, seriously, as his listener chose, he said that he had noticed how in the great department stores where nearly everything to supply human need was sold, the shopmen and shopwomen seemed instructed by the ownership or the management to deal in absolute good faith with the customers, and not to misrepresent the quality, the make, or the material of any article in the slightest degree. A thing was not to be called silk or wool when it was partly cotton; it was not to be said that it would wash when it would not wash, or that the color would not come off when it would come off, or that the stuff was English or French when it was American.

When Erlcort once noted his interest in the fact to a floor-walker whom he happened to find at leisure, the floor-walker said, Yes, that was so; and the house did it because it was business, good business, the only good business. He was instantly enthusiastic, and he said that just in the same way, as an extension of its good faith with the public, the house had established the rule of taking back any article which a customer did not like, or did not find what she had supposed when she got it home, and refunding the money. This was the best sort of business; it held custom; the woman became a customer for life. The floor-walker laughed, and after he had told an anxious applicant, "Second aisle to the left, lady; three counters back," he concluded to Erlcort, "I say she because a man never brings a thing back when he's made a mistake; but a woman can always blame it on the house. That so?"

Erlcort laughed with him, and in going out he stopped at the book-counter. Rather it was a bookstore, and no small one, with ranks of new books covering the large tables and mounting to their level from the floor, neatly piled, and with shelves of complete editions and soberer-looking volumes stretching along the wall as high as the ceiling. "Do you happen to have a good book—a book that would read good, I mean—in your stock here?" he asked the neat blonde behind the literary barricade.

"Well, here's a book that a good many are reading," she answered, with prompt interest and a smile that told in the book's favor; it was a protectingly filial and guardedly ladylike smile.

"Yes, but is it a book worth reading—worth the money?"

"Well, I don't know as I'm a judge," the kind little blonde replied. She added, daringly, "All I can say is, I set up till two last night to finish it."

"And you advise me to buy it?"

"Well, we're not allowed to do that, exactly. I can only tell you what I know."

"But if I take it, and it isn't what I expected, I can return it and get my money back?"

"That's something I never was asked before. Mr. Jeffers! Mr. Jeffers!" she called to a floor-walker passing near; and when he stopped and came up to the counter, she put the case to him.

He took the book from Erlcort's hand and examined the outside of it curiously if not critically. Then he looked from it to Erlcort, and said, "Oh, how do you do again! Well, no, sir; I don't know as we could do that. You see, you would have to read it to find out that you didn't want it, and that would be like using or wearing an article, wouldn't it? We couldn't take back a thing that had been used or worn—heigh?"

"But you might have some means of knowing whether a book is good or not?"

"Well, yes, we might. That's a point we have never had raised before. Miss Prittiman, haven't we any means of knowing whether a book's something we can guarantee or not?"

"Well, Mr. Jeffers, there's the publisher's advertisement."

"Why, yes, so there is! And a respectable publisher wouldn't indorse a book that wasn't the genuine article, would he now, sir?"

"He mightn't," Erlcort said, as if he felt the force of the argument.

"And there are the notices in the newspapers. They ought to tell," Miss Prittiman added, more convincingly. "I don't know," she said, as from a sensitive conscience, "whether there have been any about this book yet, but I should think there would be."

"And in the mean time, as you won't guarantee the book so that I can bring it back and get my money if I find it worthless, I must accept the publisher's word?" Erlcort pressed further.

"I should think you could do that," the floor-walker suggested, with the appearance of being tired.

"Well, I think I will, for once," Erlcort relented. "But wait! What does the publisher say?"

"It's all printed on this slip inside," the blonde said, and she showed it as she took the book from him. "Shall I send it? Or will you—"

"No, no, thank you, I'll take it with me. Let me—"

He kept the printed slip and began to read it. The blonde wrapped the book up and laid it with a half-dollar in change on the counter before Erlcort. The floor-walker went away; Erlcort heard him saying, "No, madam; toys on the fifth floor, at the extreme rear, left," while he lost himself in the glowing promises of the publisher. It appeared that the book he had just bought was by a perfectly new author, an old lady of seventy who had never written a novel before, and might therefore be trusted for an entire freshness of thought and feeling. The plot was of a gripping intensity; the characters were painted with large, bold strokes, and were of an unexampled virility; the story was packed with passion from cover to cover; and the reader would be held breathless by the author's skill in working from the tragic conditions to an all-round happy conclusion.

From time to time Erlcort heard the gentle blonde saying such things as, "Oh yes; it's the best-seller, all right," and, "All I can say is I set up till two o'clock in the morning to finish it," and, "Yes, ma'am; it's by a new writer; a very old lady of seventy who is just beginning to write; well, that's what I heard."

On his way up-town in the Subway he clung to the wonted strap, unsupported by anything in the romance which he had bought; and yet he could not take the book back and get his money, or even exchange it for some article of neckwear or footwear. In his extremity he thought he would try giving it to the trainman just before he reached his stop.

"You want to give it to me? Well, that's something that never happened to me on this line before. I guess my wife will like it. I——th Street! Change for East Brooklyn and the Bronx!" the guard shouted, and he let Erlcort out of the car, the very first of the tide that spilled itself forth at the station. He called after him, "Do as much for you some time."

The incident first amused Erlcort, and then it began to trouble him; but he appeased his remorse by toying with his old notion of a critical bookstore. His mind was still at play with it when he stopped at the bell-pull of an elderly girl of his acquaintance who had a studio ten stories above, and the habit of giving him afternoon tea in it if he called there about five o'clock. She had her ugly painting-apron still on, and her thumb through the hole in her palette, when she opened her door to him.

"Too soon?" he asked.

She answered as well as she could with the brush held horizontally in her mouth while she glared inhospitably at him. "Well, not much," and then she let him in, and went and lighted her spirit-lamp.

He began at once to tell her of his strange experience, and went on till she said: "Well, there's your tea. I don't know what you've been driving at, but I suppose you do. Is it the old thing?"

"It's my critical bookstore, if that's what you call the old thing."

"Oh! That! I thought it had failed 'way back in the dark ages."

"The dark ages are not back, please; they're all 'round, and you know very well that my critical bookstore has never been tried yet. But tell me one thing: should you wish to live with a picture, even for a few hours, which had been painted by an old lady of seventy who had never tried to paint before?"

"If I intended to go crazy, yes. What has all that got to do with it?"

"That's the joint commendation of the publisher and the kind little blonde who united to sell me the book I just gave to that poor Subway trainman. Do you ever buy a new book?"

"No; I always borrow an old one."

"But if you had to buy a new one, wouldn't you like to know of a place where you could be sure of getting a good one?"

"I shouldn't mind. Or, yes, I should, rather. Where's it to be?"

"Oh, I know. I've had my eye on the place for a good while. It's a funny old place in Sixth Avenue—"

"Sixth Avenue!"

"Don't interrupt—where the dearest old codger in the world is just going out of the house-furnishing business in a small way. It's kept getting smaller and smaller—I've watched it shrink—till now it can't stand up against the big shops, and the old codger told me the other day that it was no use."

"Poor fellow!"

"No. He's not badly off, and he's going back up-state where he came from about forty years ago, and he can live—or die—very well on what he's put by. I've known him rather a good while, and we've been friends ever since we've been acquainted."

"Go on," the elderly girl said.

Erlcort was not stopping, but she spoke so as to close her mouth, which she was apt to let hang open in a way that she did not like; she had her intimates pledged to tell her when she was doing it, but she could not make a man promise, and she had to look after her mouth herself with Erlcort. It was not a bad mouth; her eyes were large, and it was merely large to match them.

"When shall you begin—open shop?" she asked.

"My old codger's lease expires in the fall," he answered, "but he would be glad to have me take it off his hands this spring. I could give the summer to changing and decorating, and begin my campaign in the fall—the first of October, say. Wouldn't you like to come some day and see the old place?"

"I should love it. But you're not supposing I shall be of the least use, I hope? I'm not decorational, you know. Easel pictures, and small ones at that."

"Of course. But you are a woman, and have ideas of the cozy. I mean that the place shall be made attractive."

"Do you think the situation will be—on Sixth Avenue?"

"It will be quaint. It's in a retarded region of low buildings, with a carpenter's shop two doors off. The L roars overhead and the surface cars squeal before, but that is New York, you know, and it's very central. Besides, at the back of the shop, with the front door shut, it is very quiet."

The next day the friends lunched together at an Italian restaurant very near the place, and rather hurried themselves away to the old codger's store.

"He is a dear," Margaret whispered to Erlcort in following him about to see the advantages of the place.

"Oh, mine's setting-hen's time," he justified his hospitality in finally asking them to take seats on a nail-keg apiece. "You mustn't think you're interruptin'. Look 'round all ye want to, or set down and rest ye."

"That would be a good motto for your bookstore," she screamed to Erlcort, when they got out into the roar of the avenue. "'Look 'round all ye want to, or set down and rest ye.' Wasn't he sweet? And I don't wonder you're taken with the place: it has such capabilities. You might as well begin imagining how you will arrange it."

They were walking involuntarily up the avenue, and when they came to the Park they went into it, and in the excitement of their planning they went as far as the Ramble, where they sat down on a bench and disappointed some squirrels who supposed they had brought peanuts with them.

They decided that the front of the shop should be elaborately simple; perhaps the door should be painted black, with a small-paned sash and a heavy brass latch. On each side should be a small-paned show-window, with books laid inside on an inclined shelving; on the door should be a modest bronze plate, reading, "The Critical Bookstore." They rejected shop as an affectation, and they hooted the notion of "Ye Critical Bookstore" as altogether loathsome. The door and window would be in a rather belated taste, but the beautiful is never out of date, and black paint and small panes might be found rococo in their old-fashionedness now. There should be a fireplace, or perhaps a Franklin stove, at the rear of the room, with a high-shouldered, small-paned sash on each side letting in the light from the yard of the carpenter-shop. On the chimneypiece should be lettered, "Look 'round all ye want to, or set down and rest ye."

The genius of the place should be a refined hospitality, such as the gentle old codger had practised with them, and to facilitate this there should be a pair of high-backed settles, one under each window. The book-counter should stretch the whole length of the store, and at intervals beside it, against the book-shelving, should be set old-fashioned chairs, but not too old-fashioned. Against the lower book-shelves on a deeper shelf might be stood against the books a few sketches in water-color, or even oil.

This was Margaret Green's idea.

"And would you guarantee the quality?" Erlcort asked.

"Perhaps they wouldn't be for sale, though if any one insisted—"

"I see. Well, pass the sketches. What else?"

"Well, a few little figures in plaster, or even marble or bronze, very Greek, or very American; things in low relief."

"Pass the little figures and low reliefs. But don't forget it's a bookstore."

"Oh, I won't. The sketches of all kinds would be strictly subordinated to the books. If I had a tea-room handy here, with a table and the backs of some menus to draw on, I could show you just how it would look."

"What's the matter with the Casino?"

"Nothing; only it's rather early for tea yet."

"It isn't for soda-lemonade."

She set him the example of instantly rising, and led the way back along the lake to the Casino, resting at that afternoon hour among its spring flowers and blossoms innocent of its lurid after-dark frequentation. He got some paper from the waiter who came to take their order. She began to draw rapidly, and by the time the waiter came again she was giving Erlcort the last scrap of paper.

"Well," he said, "I had no idea that I had imagined anything so charming! If this critical bookstore doesn't succeed, it'll be because there are no critics. But what—what are these little things hung against the partitions of the shelves?"

"Oh—mirrors. Little round ones."

"But why mirrors of any shape?"

"Nothing; only people like to see themselves in a glass of any shape. And when," Margaret added, in a burst of candor, "a woman looks up and sees herself with a book in her hand, she will feel so intellectual she will never put it down. She will buy it."

"Margaret Green, this is immoral. Strike out those mirrors, or I will smash them every one!"

"Oh, very well!" she said, and she rubbed them out with the top of her pencil. "If you want your place a howling wilderness."

He looked at the ruin her rubber had wrought. "They were rather nice. Could —could you rub them in again?"

"Not if I tried a hundred years. Besides, they were rather impudent. What time is it?"

"No time at all. It's half-past three."

"Dear me! I must be going. And if you're really going to start that precious critical bookstore in the fall, you must begin work on it right away."

"Work?"

"Reading up for it. If you're going to guarantee the books, you must know what's in them, mustn't you?"

He realized that he must do what she said; he must know from his own knowledge what was in the books he offered for sale, and he began reading, or reading at, the new books immediately. He was a good deal occupied by day with the arrangement of his store, though he left it mainly with the lively young decorator who undertook for a lump sum to realize Margaret Green's ideas. It was at night that he did most of his reading in the spring books which the publishers were willing to send him gratis, when they understood he was going to open a bookstore, and only wanted sample copies. As long as she remained in town Margaret Green helped him read, and they talked the books over, and mostly rejected them. By the time she went to Europe in August with another elderly girl they had not chosen more than eight or ten books; but they hoped for better things in the fall.

Word of what he was doing had gone out from Margaret, and a great many women of their rather esthetic circle began writing to him about the books they were reading, and commending them to him or warning him against them. The circle of his volunteer associates enlarged itself in the nature of an endless chain, and before society quite broke up for the summer a Sympathetic Tea was offered to Erlcort by a Leading Society Woman at the Intellectual Club, where he was invited to address the Intellectuals in explanation of his project. This was before Margaret sailed, and he hurried to her in horror.

"Why, of course you must accept. You're not going to hide your Critical Bookstore under a bushel; you can't have too much publicity."

The Leading Society Woman flowed in fulsome gratitude at his acceptance, and promised no one but the club should be there; he had hinted his reluctance. She kept her promise, but among the Intellectuals there was a girl who was a just beginning journalist, and who pumped Erlcort's whole scheme out of him, unsuspicious of what she was doing, till he saw it all, with his picture, in the Sunday Supplement. She rightly judged that the intimacy of an interview would be more popular with her readers than the cold and distant report of his formal address, which she must give, though she received it so ardently with all the other Intellectuals. They flocked flatteringly, almost suffocatingly, around him at the end. His scheme was just what every one had vaguely thought of: something must be done to stem the tide of worthless fiction, which was so often shocking as well as silly, and they would only be too glad to help read for him. They were nearly all just going to sail, but they would each take a spring book on the ship, and write him about it from the other side; they would each get a fall book coming home, and report as soon as they got back.

His scheme was discussed seriously and satirically by the press; it became a joke with many papers, and a byword quickly worn out, so that people thought that it had been dropped. But Erlcort gave his days and nights to preparation for his autumnal campaign. He studied in careful comparison the reviews of the different literary authorities, and was a little surprised to find, when he came to read the books they reviewed, how honest and adequate they often were. He was obliged to own to himself that if people were guided by them, few worthless books would be sold, and he decided that the immense majority of the book-buyers were not guided by the critics. The publishers themselves seemed not so much to blame when he went to see them and explained his wish to deal with them on the basis of a critical bookseller. They said they wished all the booksellers were like him, for they would ask nothing better than to publish only good books. The trouble, they said, lay with the authors; they wrote such worthless books. Or if now and then one of them did write a good book and they were over-tempted to publish it, the public united in refusing to buy it. So he saw? But if the booksellers persisted in selling none but good books, perhaps something might be done. At any rate they would like to see the experiment tried.

Erlcort felt obliged to read the books suggested to him by the endless chain of readers who volunteered to read for him, on both sides of the ocean, or going and coming on the ocean. Mostly the books they praised were abject rubbish, but it took time to find this out, and he formed the habit of reading far into the night, and if he was very much vexed at discovering that the book recommended to him was trash, he could not sleep unless he took veronal, and then he had a ghastly next day.

He did not go out of town except for a few brief sojourns at places where he knew cultivated people were staying, and could give him their opinions of the books he was reading. When the publishers began, as they had agreed, to send him their advance sheets, the stitched but unbound volumes roused so much interest by the novelty of their form that his readers could not give an undivided attention to their contents. He foresaw that in the end he should have to rely upon the taste of mercenaries in his warfare against rubbish, and more and more he found it necessary to expend himself in it, to read at second hand as well as at first. His greatest relief was in returning to town and watching the magical changes which the decorator was working in his store. This was consolation, this was inspiration, but he longed for the return of Margaret Green, that she might help him enjoy the realization of her ideas in the equipment of the place; and he held the decorator to the most slavish obedience through the carpenters and painters who created at his bidding a miraculous interior, all white, or just off-white, such as had never been imagined of a bookstore in New York before. It was actually ready by the end of August, though smelling a little of turpentine still, and Erlcort, letting himself in at the small-paned black door, and ranging up and down the long, beautiful room, and round and round the central book-table, and in and out between the side tables, under the soft, bright shelving of the walls, could hardly wait the arrival of the Minnedingdong in which the elderly girl had taken her passage back. One day, ten days ahead of time, she blew in at the front door in a paroxysm of explanation; she had swapped passages home with another girl who wanted to come back later, while she herself wanted to come back earlier. She had no very convincing reason for this as she gave it, but Erlcort did not listen to her reason, whatever it was. He said, between the raptures with the place that she fell in and out of, that now she was just in time for the furnishing, which he never could have dared to undertake alone.

In the gay September weather they visited all the antiquity shops in Fourth Avenue, and then threw themselves frankly upon reproductions, which they bought in the native wood and ordered painted, the settles and the spindle-backed chairs in the cool gray which she decided was the thing. In the same spirit they bought new brass fire-irons and new shovel and tongs, but all very tall and antique-looking, and then they got those little immoral mirrors, which Margaret Green attached with her own hands to the partitions of the shelving. She also got soft green silk curtains for the chimney windows and for the sash of the front door; even the front windows she curtained, but very low, so that a salesman or a saleswoman could easily reach over from the interior and get a book that any customer had seen from the outside.

One day when all this was done, and Erlcort had begun ordering in a stock of such books as he had selected to start with, she said: "You're looking rather peakéd, aren't you?"

"Well, I've been feeling rather peakéd, until lately, keeping awake to read and read after the volunteer readers."

"You mean you've lost sleep?"

"Something like that."

"Well, you mustn't. How many books do you start with?"

"About twenty-five."

"Good ones? It's a lot, isn't it? I didn't suppose there were so many."

"Well, to fill our shelves I shall have to order about a thousand of each."

"You'll never sell them in the world! You'll be ruined."

"Oh no; the publishers will take them back."

"How nice of them! But that's only what painters have to do when the dealers can't sell their pictures."

A month off, the prospect was brilliant, and when the shelves and tables were filled and the sketches and bas-reliefs were stuck about and the little immoral mirrors were hung, the place was charming. The chairs and settles were all that could be asked; Margaret Green helped put them about; and he let her light the low fire on the hearth of the Franklin stove; he said he should not always burn hickory, but he had got twenty-four sticks for two dollars from an Italian in a cellar near by, and he meant to burn that much. She upbraided him for his extravagance while touching the match to the paper under the kindling; but October opened cold, and he needed the fire.

The enterprise seemed rather to mystify the neighborhood, and some old customers of the old codger's came in upon one fictitious errand and another to see about it, and went away without quite making it out. It was a bookstore, all right, they owned in conference, but what did he mean by "critical"?

The first bona fide buyer appeared in a little girl who could just get her chin on the counter, and who asked for an egg-beater. Erlcort had begun with only one assistant, the young lady who typed his letters and who said she guessed she could help him when she was not working. She leaned over and tried to understand the little girl, and then she called to Erlcort where he stood with his back to the fire and the morning paper open before his face.

"Mr. Erlcort, have we got a book called The Egg-beater?"

"The Egg-beater?" he echoed, letting his paper drop below his face.

"No, no!" the little girl shouted, angrily. "It ain't a book. It's a thing to beat eggs with. Mother said to come here and get it."

"Well, she's sent you to the wrong place, little girl. You want to go to a hardware-store," the young lady argued.

"Ain't this No. ?"

"Yes."

"Well, this is the right place. Mother said to go to . I guess she knows. She's an old customer."

"The Egg-beater! The Egg-beater!" the blithe young novelist to whom Erlcort told the story repeated. He was still happy in his original success as a best-seller, and he had come to the Critical Bookstore to spy out the stock and see whether his last novel was in it; but though it was not, he joyously extended an acquaintance with Erlcort which had begun elsewhere. "The Egg-beater? What a splendid title for a story of adventure! Keep the secret of its applicability to the last word, or perhaps never reveal it at all, and leave the reader worrying. That's one way; makes him go and talk about the book to all the girls he knows and get them guessing. Best ad. in the world. The Egg-beater! Doesn't it suggest desert islands and penguins' nests in the rocks? Fellow and girl shipwrecked, and girl wants to make an omelette after they've got sick of plain eggs, and can't for want of an egg-beater. Heigh? He invents one—makes it out of some wire that floats off from the wreck. See? When they are rescued, she brings it away, and doesn't let him know it till their Iron Wedding Day. They keep it over his study fireplace always."

This author was the first to stretch his legs before Erlcort's fire from his seat on one of the reproductions. He could not say enough of the beauty of the place, and he asked if he might sit there and watch for the old codger's old customers coming to buy hardware. There might be copy in it.

But the old customers did not come so often as he hoped and Erlcort feared. Instead there came bona fide book-buyers, who asked some for a book and some for a particular book. The first were not satisfied with the books that Erlcort or his acting saleslady recommended, and went away without buying. The last were indignant at not finding what they wanted in Erlcort's selection.

"Why don't you stock it?" they demanded.

"Because I don't think it's worth reading."

"Oh, indeed!" The sarcastic customers were commonly ladies. "I thought you let the public judge of that!"

"There are bookstores where they do. This is a critical bookstore. I sell only the books that I think worth reading. If you had noticed my sign—"

"Oh!" the customer would say, and she, too, would go away without buying.

There were other ladies who came, links of the endless chain of volunteer readers who had tried to help Erlcort in making his selection, and he could see them slyly looking his stock over for the books they had praised to him. Mostly they went away without comment, but with heads held high in the offense which he felt even more than saw. One, indeed, did ask him why he had not stocked her chosen book, and he had to say, "Well, when I came to go through it carefully, I didn't think it quite—"

"But here is The Green Bay Tree, and The Biggest Toad in the Puddle, and—"

"I know. For one reason and another I thought them worth stocking."

Then another head went away high in the air, with its plumes quivering. One afternoon late a lady came flying in with all the marks, whatever they are, of transatlantic travel upon her.

"I'm just through the customs, and I've motored up here the first thing, even before I went home, to stop you from selling that book I recommended. It's dreadful; and, horrors! horrors! here it is by the hundreds! Oh, Mr. Erlcort! You mustn't sell that dreadful book! You see, I had skipped through it in my berth going out, and posted my letter the first thing; and just now, coming home, I found it in the ship's library and came on that frightful episode. You know! Where— How could you order it without reading it, on a mere say-so? It's utterly immoral!"

"I don't agree with you," Erlcort answered, dryly. "I consider that passage one of the finest in modern fiction—one of the most ennobling and illumining—"

"Ennobling!" The lady made a gesture of horror. "Very well! If that is your idea of a critical bookstore, all I've got to say is—"

But she had apparently no words to say it in, and she went out banging but failing to latch the door which let through the indignant snort of her car as it whirled her away. She left Erlcort and his assistant to a common silence, but he imagined somehow a resolution in the stenographer not to let the book go unsearched till she had grasped the full iniquity of that episode and felt all its ennobling force. He was not consoled when another lady came in and, after drifting unmolestedly about (it was the primary rule of the place not to follow people up), stopped before the side shelf where the book was ranged in dozens and scores. She took a copy from the neat ranks, and opened it; then she lifted her head by chance and caught sight of her plume in one of the little mirrors.

She stealthily lifted herself on tiptoe till she could see her face, and then she turned to the assistant and said, gently, "I believe I should like this book, please," and paid for it and went out.

It was now almost on the stroke of six, and Erlcort said to his assistant: "I'll close the store, Miss Pearsall. You needn't stay any longer."

"All right, sir," the girl said, and went into the little closet at the rear for her hat and coat. Did she contrive to get a copy of that book under her coat as she passed the shelf where it lay?

When she was gone, he turned the key in the door and went back and sat down before the fire dying on the hearth of the Franklin stove. It was not a very cheerful moment with him, but he could not have said that the day had been unprofitable, either spiritually or pecuniarily. In its experiences it had been a varied day, and he had really sold a good many books. More people than he could have expected had taken him seriously and even intelligently. It is true that he had been somewhat vexed by the sort of authority the president of the Intellectual Club had shown in the way she swelled into the store and patronized him and it, as if she had invented them both, and blamed him in a high, sweet voice for having so many old books. "My idea was that it would be a place where one could come for the best of the new books. But here! Why, half of them I saw in June before I sailed!" She chided him merrily, and she acted as if it were quite part of the joke when he said that he did not think a good book could age much in four months. She laughed patronizingly at his conceit of getting in the fall books by Thanksgiving; but even for the humor of it she could not let him say he should not do anything in holiday books. "I had expected to get all my Christmas books of you, Mr. Erlcort," she crowed, but for the present she bought nothing. In compensation he recalled the gratitude, almost humble gratitude, of a lady (she was a lady!) who had come that day, bringing her daughter to get a book, any book in his stock, and to thank him for his enterprise, which she had found worked perfectly in the case of the book she had got the week before; the book had been an unalloyed delight, and had left a sense of heightened self-respect with her: that book of the dreadful episode.

He wished Margaret Green had been there; but she had been there only once since his opening; he could not think why. He heard a rattling at the door-latch, and he said before he turned to look, "What if it should be she now?" But when he went to peer through the door-curtain it was only an old fellow who had spent the better part of the afternoon in the best chair, reading a book. Erlcort went back to the fire and let him rattle, which he did rather a long time, and then went away, Erlcort hoped, in dudgeon. He was one of a number of customers who had acted on the half of his motto asking them to sit down and rest them, after acting on the other half to look round all they wanted. Most of them did not read, even; they seemed to know one another, and they talked comfortably together. Erlcort recognized a companionship of four whom he had noticed in the Park formerly; they were clean-enough-looking elderly men, but occupied nearly all the chairs and settles, so that lady customers did not like to bring books and look over them in the few places left, and Erlcort foresaw the time when he should have to ask the old fellows to look around more and rest them less. In resuming his own place before the fire he felt the fleeting ache of a desire to ask Margaret Green whether it would not be a good plan to remove the motto from the chimneypiece. He would not have liked to do it without asking her; it had been her notion to put it there, and her other notion of the immoral mirrors had certainly worked well. The thoughtful expression they had reflected on the faces of lady customers had sold a good many books; not that Erlcort wished to sell books that way, though he argued with himself that his responsibility ought strictly to end with the provision of books which he had critically approved before offering them for sale.

His conscience was not wholly at peace as to his stock, not only the books which he had included, but also those he had excluded. Some of these tacitly pleaded against his severity; in one case an author came and personally protested. This was the case of a book by the ex-best-seller, who held that his last book was so much better than his first that it ought certainly to be found in any critical bookstore. The proceeds of his best-seller had enabled him to buy an electric runabout, and he purred up to Erlcort's door in it to argue the matter with him. He sat down in a reproduction and proved, gaily, that Erlcort was quite wrong about it. He had the book with him, and read passages from it; then he read passages from some of the books on sale and defied Erlcort to say that his passages were not just as good, or, as he put it merrily, the same as. He held that his marked improvement entitled him to the favor of a critical bookstore; without this, what motive had he in keeping from a reversion to the errors which had won him the vicious prosperity of his first venture? Hadn't Erlcort a duty to perform in preventing his going back to the bad? Refuse this markedly improved fiction, and you drove him to writing nothing but best-sellers from now on. He urged Erlcort to reflect.

They had a jolly time, and the ex-best-seller went away in high spirits, prophesying that Erlcort would come to his fiction yet.

There were authors who did not leave Erlcort so cheerful when they failed to see their books on his shelves or tables. Some of them were young authors who had written their worthless books with a devout faith in their worth, and they went away more in sorrow than in anger, and yet more in bewilderment. Some were old authors who had been all their lives acceptably writing second-rate books and trying to make them unacceptably first-rate. If he knew them he kept out of their way, but the dejection of their looks was not less a pang to him if he saw them searching his stock for their books in vain.

He had his own moments of dejection. The interest of the press in his enterprise had flashed through the Sunday issues of a single week, and then flashed out in lasting darkness. He wondered vaguely if he had counted without the counting-house in hoping for their continued favor; he could not realize that nothing is so stale as old news, and that no excess of advertising would have relumed those fitful fires.

He would have liked to talk the case over with Margaret Green. After his first revolt from the easy publicity the reporters had first given him, he was aware of having enjoyed it—perhaps vulgarly enjoyed it. But he hoped not quite that; he hoped that in his fleeting celebrity he had cared for his scheme rather than himself. He had really believed in it, and he liked having it recognized as a feature of modern civilization, an innovation which did his city and his country credit. Now and then an essayist of those who wrote thoughtful articles in the Sunday or Saturday-evening editions had dropped in, and he had opened his heart to them in a way he would not have minded their taking advantage of. Secretly he hoped they would see a topic in his enterprise and his philosophy of it. But they never did, and he was left to the shame of hopes which had held nothing to support defeat. He would have liked to confess his shame and own the justice of his punishment to Margaret Green, but she seemed the only friend who never came near. Other friends came, and many strangers, the friends to look and the strangers to buy. He had no reason to complain of his sales; the fame of his critical bookstore might have ceased in New York, because it had gone abroad to Chicago and St. Louis and Pittsburg; people who were clearly from these commercial capitals and others came and bought copiously of his criticized stock, and they praised the notion of it in telling him that he ought to open branches in their several cities.

They were all women, and it was nearly all women who frequented the Critical Bookstore, but in their multitude Margaret Green was not. He thought it the greater pity because she would have enjoyed many of them with him, and would have divined such as hoped the culture implicated by a critical bookstore would come off on them without great effort of their own; she would have known the sincere spirits, too, and could have helped direct their choice of the best where all was so good. He smiled to find that he was invoking her help, which he had no right to.

His longing had no effect upon her till deep in January, when the weather was engaged late one afternoon in keeping the promise of a January thaw in the form of the worst snow-storm of the winter. Then she came thumping with her umbrella-handle at his door as if, he divined, she were too stiff-handed or too package-laden to press the latch and let herself in, and she almost fell in, but saved herself by spilling on the floor some canvases and other things which she had been getting at the artist's-materials store near by. "Don't bother about them," she said, "but take me to the fire as fast as you can," and when she had turned from snow to rain and had dripped partially dry before the Franklin stove, she asked, "Where have you been all the time?"

"Waiting here for you," he answered.

"Well, you needn't. I wasn't going to come—or at least not till you sent for me, or said you wanted my advice."

"I don't want your advice now."

"I didn't come to give it. I just dropped in because if I hadn't I should have just dropped outside. How have you been getting along with your ridiculous critical bookstore?"

"Well, things are rather quiet with us just now, as the publishers say to the authors when they don't want to publish their books."

"Yes, I know that saying. Why didn't you go in for the holiday books?"

"How did you know I didn't?"

"Lots of people told me."

"Well, then, I'll tell you why. I would have had to read them first, and no human being could do that—not even a volunteer link in an endless chain."

"I see. But since Christmas?"

"You know very well that after Christmas the book market drops dead."

"Yes, so I've been told." She had flung her wet veil back over her shoulders, and he thought she had never looked so adorably plain before; if she could have seen herself in a glass she would have found her whole face out of drawing. It seemed as if his thinking had put her in mind of them, and she said, "Those immoral mirrors are shameful."

"They've sold more of the best books than anything else."

"No matter. As soon as I get a little drier I shall take them down."

"Very well. I didn't put them up." He laid a log of hickory on the fire. "I'm not doing it to dry you quicker."

"Oh, I know. I'll tell you one thing. You ought to keep the magazines, or at least the Big Four. You could keep them with a good conscience, and you could sell them without reading; they're always good."

"There's an idea in that. I believe I'll try it."

Margaret Green was now dry enough, and she rose and removed the mirrors. In doing this she noticed that Erlcort had apparently sold a good many of his best books, and she said: "Well! I don't see why you should be discouraged."

"Who said I was? I'm exultant."

"Then you were exulting with the corners of your mouth down just now. Well, I must be going. Will you get a taxi to flounder over to the Subway with me?" While Erlcort was telephoning she was talking to him. "I believe the magazines will revive public interest in your scheme. Put them in your window. Try to get advance copies for it."

"You have a commercial genius, Margaret Green."

"When it comes to selling literature, I have. Selling art is where I fall down."

"That's because you always try to sell your own art. I should fall down, too, if I tried to sell my own literature."

They got quite back to their old friendliness; the coming of the taxi gave them plenty of time. The electric lights were turned brilliantly on, but there, at the far end of the store, before the Franklin stove, they had a cozy privacy. At the moment of parting she said:

"If I were you I should take out these settles. They simply invite loafing."

"I've noticed that they seem to do that."

"And better paint out that motto."

"I've sometimes fancied I'd better. That invites loafing, too; though some nice people like it."

"Nice people? Why haven't some of them bought a picture?" He perceived that she had taken in the persistent presence of the sketches when removing the mirrors, and he shared the indignation she expressed: "Shabby things!"

She stood with the mirrors under her arm, and he asked what she was going to do with them, as he followed her to the door with her other things.

"Put them around the studio. But you needn't come to see the effect."

"No. I shall come to see you."

But when he came in a lull of February, and he could walk part of the way up through the Park on the sunny Saturday afternoon, she said:

"I suppose you've come to pour out some more of your griefs. Well, pour away! Has the magazine project failed?"

"On the contrary, it has been a succès fou. But I don't feel altogether easy in my mind about it. The fact is, they seem to print much more rubbish than I supposed."

"Of course they do; they must; rubbish is the breath in their nostrils."

She painted away, screwing her eyes almost shut and getting very close to her picture. He had never thought her so plain; she was letting her mouth hang open. He wondered why she was so charming; but when she stepped back rhythmically, tilting her pretty head this way and that, he saw why: it was her unfailing grace. She suddenly remembered her mouth and shut it to say, "Well?"

"Well, some people have come back at me. They've said, What a rotten number this or that was! They were right; and yet there were things in all those magazines better than anything they had ever printed. What's to be done about it? I can't ask people to buy truck or read truck because it comes bound up with essays and stories and poems of the first quality."

"No. You can't. Why," she asked, drifting up to her picture again, "don't you tear the bad out, and sell the good?"

Erlcort gave a disdainful sound, such as cannot be spelled in English. "Do you know how defiantly the bad is bound up with the good in the magazines? They're wired together, and you could no more tear out the bad and leave the good than you could part vice from virtue in human nature."

"I see," Margaret Green said, but she saw no further, and she had to let him go disconsolate. After waiting a decent time she went to find him in his critical bookstore. It was late in an afternoon of the days that were getting longer, and only one electric was lighted in the rear of the room, where Erlcort sat before the fireless Franklin stove, so busy at something that he scarcely seemed aware of her.

"What in the world are you doing?" she demanded.

He looked up. "Who? I? Oh, it's you! Why, I'm merely censoring the truck in the May number of this magazine." He held up a little roller, as long as the magazine was wide, blacked with printer's ink, which he had been applying to the open periodical. "I've taken a hint from the way the Russian censorship blots out seditious literature before it lets it go to the public."

"And what a mess you're making!"

"Of course it will have to dry before it's put on sale."

"I should think so. Listen to me, Frederick Erlcort: you're going crazy."

"I've sometimes thought so: crazy with conceit and vanity and arrogance. Who am I that I should set up for a critical bookstore-keeper? What is the Republic of Letters, anyway? A vast, benevolent, generous democracy, where one may have what one likes, or a cold oligarchy where he is compelled to take what is good for him? Is it a restricted citizenship, with a minority representation, or is it universal suffrage?"

"Now," Margaret Green said, "you are talking sense. Why didn't you think of this in the beginning?"

"Is it a world, a whole earth," he went on, "where the weeds mostly outflourish the flowers, or is it a wretched little florist's conservatory where the watering-pot assumes to better the instruction of the rain which falls upon the just and the unjust? What is all the worthy family of asses to do if there are no thistles to feed them? Because the succulent fruits and nourishing cereals are better for the finer organisms, are the coarser not to have fodder? No; I have made a mistake. Literature is the whole world; it is the expression of the gross, the fatuous, and the foolish, and it is the pleasure of the gross, the fatuous, and the foolish, as well as the expression and the pleasure of the wise, the fine, the elect. Let the multitude have their truck, their rubbish, their rot; it may not be the truck, the rubbish, the rot that it would be to us, or may slowly and by natural selection become to certain of them. But let there be no artificial selection, no survival of the fittest by main force—the force of the spectator, who thinks he knows better than the creator of the ugly and the beautiful, the fair and foul, the evil and good."

"Oh, now if the Intellectual Club could hear you!" Margaret Green said, with a long, deep, admiring suspiration. "And what are you going to do with your critical bookstore?"

"I'm going to sell it. I've had an offer from the author of that best-seller—I've told you about him. I was just trying to censor that magazine while I was thinking it over. He's got an idea. He's going to keep it a critical bookstore, but the criticism is to be made by universal suffrage and the will of the majority. The latest books will be put to a vote; and the one getting the greatest number of votes will be the first offered for sale, and the author will receive a free passage to Europe by the southern route."

"The southern route!" Margaret mused. "I've never been that way. It must be delightful."

"Then come with me! I'm going."

"But how can I?"

"By marrying me!"

"I never thought of that," she said. Then, with the conscientious resolution of an elderly girl who puts her fate to the touch of any risk the truth compels, she added: "Or, yes! I have. But I never supposed you would ask me." She stared at him, and she was aware she was letting her mouth hang open. While she was trying for some word to close it with he closed it for her.

XIV
A FEAST OF REASON

Florindo and Lindora had come to the end of another winter in town, and had packed up for another summer in the country. They were sitting together over their last breakfast until the taxi should arrive to whirl them away to the station, and were brooding in a joint gloom from the effect of the dinner they had eaten at the house of a friend the night before, and, "Well, thank goodness," she said, "there is an end to that sort of thing for one while."

"An end to that thing," he partially assented, "but not that sort of thing."

"What do you mean?" she demanded excitedly, almost resentfully.

"I mean that the lunch is of the nature of the dinner, and that in the country we shall begin lunching where we left off dining."

"Not instantly," she protested shrilly. "There will be nobody there for a while —not for a whole month, nearly."

"They will be there before you can turn round, almost; and then you women will begin feeding one another there before you have well left off here."

"We women!" she protested.

"Yes, you—you women. You give the dinners. Can you deny it?"

"It's because we can't get you to the lunches."

"In the country you can; and so you will give the lunches."

"We would give dinners if it were not for the distance, and the darkness on those bad roads."

"I don't see where your reasoning is carrying you."

"No," she despaired, "there is no reason in it. No sense. How tired of it all I am! And, as you say, it will be no time before it is all going on again."

They computed the number of dinners they had given during the winter; that was not hard, and the sum was not great: six or seven at the most, large and small. When it came to the dinners they had received, it was another thing; but still she considered, "Were they really so few? It's nothing to what the English do. They never dine alone at home, and they never dine alone abroad—of course not! I wonder they can stand it. I think a dinner, the happy-to-accept kind, is always loathsome: the everlasting soup, if there aren't oysters first, or grape-fruit, or melon, and the fish, and the entrée, and the roast and salad, and the ice-cream and the fruit nobody touches, and the coffee and cigarettes and cigars—how I hate it all!"

Lindora sank back in her chair and toyed desperately with the fragment of bacon on her plate.

"And yet," Florindo said, "there is a charm about the first dinner of autumn, after you've got back."

"Oh, yes," she assented; "it's like a part of our lost youth. We think all the dinners of the winter will be like that, and we come away beaming."

"But when it keeps on and there's more and more of our lost youth, till it comes to being the whole—"

"Florindo!" she stopped him. He pretended that he was not going to have said it, and she resumed, dreamily, "I wonder what it is makes it so detestable as the winter goes on."

"All customs are detestable, the best of them," he suggested, "and I should say, in spite of the first autumnal dinner, that the society dinner was an unlovely rite. You try to carry if off with china and glass, and silver and linen, and if people could fix their minds on these, or even on the dishes of the dinner as they come successively on, it would be all very well; but the diners, the diners!"

"Yes," she said, "the old men are hideous, certainly; and the young ones—I try not to look at them, poking things into the hollows of their faces with spoons and forks—"

"Better than when it was done with knives! Still, it's a horror! A veteran diner-out in full action is certainly a hideous spectacle. Often he has few teeth of his own, and the dentists don't serve him perfectly. He is in danger of dropping things out of his mouth, both liquids and solids: better not look! His eyes bulge and roll in his head in the stress of mastication and deglutition; his color rises and spreads to his gray hair or over his baldness; his person seems to swell vividly in his chair, and when he laughs—"

"Don't, Florindo! It is awful."

"Well, perhaps no worse than the sight of a middle-aged matron tending to overweight and bulking above her plate—"

"Yes, yes! That's dreadful, too. But when people are young—"

"Oh, when people are young!" He said this in despair. Then he went on in an audible muse. "When people are young they are not only in their own youth; they are in the youth of the world, the race. They dine, but they don't think of the dinner or the unpleasantness of the diners, and the grotesqueness of feeding in common. They think—" he broke off in defect of other ideas, and concluded with a laugh, "they think of themselves. And they don't think of how they are looking."

"They needn't; they are looking very well. Don't keep harping on that! I remember when we first began going to dinners, I thought it was the most beautiful thing in the world. I don't mean when I was a girl; a girl only goes to a dinner because it comes before a dance. I mean when we were young married people; and I pinned up my dress and we went in the horse-cars, or even walked. I enjoyed every instant of it: the finding who was going to take me in and who you were; and the going in; and the hovering round the table to find our places from the cards; and the seeing how you looked next some one else, and wondering how you thought I looked; and the beads sparkling up through the champagne and getting into one's nose; and the laughing and joking and talking! Oh, the talking! What's become of it? The talking, last night, it bored me to death! And what good stories people used to tell, women as well as men! You can't deny it was beautiful."

"I don't; and I don't deny that the forms of dining are still charming. It's the dining itself that I object to."

"That's because your digestion is bad."

"Isn't yours?"

"Of course it is. What has that got to do with it?"

"It seems to me that we have arrived at what is called an impasse in French." He looked up at the clock on the wall, and she gave a little jump in her chair. "Oh, there's plenty of time. The taxi won't be here for half an hour yet. Is there any heat left in that coffee?"

"There will be," she said, and she lighted the lamp under the pot. "But I don't like being scared out of half a year's growth."

"I'm sorry. I won't look at the clock any more; I don't care if we're left. Where were we? Oh, I remember—the objection to dining itself. If we could have the forms without the facts, dining would be all right. Our superstition is that we can't be gay without gorging; that society can't be run without meat and drink. But don't you remember when we first went to Italy there was no supper at Italian houses where we thought it such a favor to be asked?"

"I remember that the young Italian swells wouldn't go to the American and English houses where they weren't sure of supper. They didn't give supper at the Italian houses because they couldn't afford it."

"I know that. I believe they do, now. But—

'Sweet are the uses of adversity,'

and the fasting made for beauty then more than the feasting does now. It was a lovelier sight to see the guests of those Italian houses conversing together without the grossness of feeding or being fed—the sort of thing one saw at our houses when people went out to supper."

"I wonder," Lindora said, "whether the same sort of thing goes on at evening parties still—it's so long since I've been at one. It was awful standing jammed up in a corner or behind a door and eating vis-à-vis with a man who brought you a plate; and it wasn't much better when you sat down and he stood over you gabbling and gobbling, with his plate in one hand and his fork in the other. I was always afraid of his dropping things into my lap; and the sight of his jaws champing as you looked up at them from below!"

"Yes, ridiculous. But there was an element of the grotesque in a bird's-eye view of a lady making shots at her mouth with a spoon and trying to smile and look spirituelle between the shots."

Lindora as she laughed bowed her forehead on the back of her hand in the way Florindo thought so pretty when they were both young. "Yes," she said, "awful, awful! Why should people want to flock together when they feed? Do you suppose it's a survival of the primitive hospitality when those who had something to eat hurried to share it with those who had nothing?"

"Possibly," Florindo said, flattered into consequence by her momentary deference, or show of it. "But the people who mostly meet to feed together now are not hungry; they are already so stuffed that they loathe the sight of the things. Some of them shirk the consequences by frankly dining at home first, and then openly or covertly dodging the courses."

"Yes, and you hear that praised as a mark of high civilization, or social wisdom. I call it wicked, and an insult to the very genius of hospitality."

"Well, I don't know. It must give the faster a good chance of seeing how funny the feeders all look."

"I wonder, I do wonder, how the feeding in common came to be the custom," she said, thoughtfully. "Of course where it's done for convenience, like hotels or in boarding-houses—but to do it wantonly, as people do in society, it ought to be stopped."

"We might call art to our aid—have a large tableful of people kodaked in the moments of ingulfing, chewing, or swallowing, as the act varied from guest to guest; might be reproduced as picture postals, or from films for the movies. That would give the ten and twenty cent audiences a chance to see what life in the exclusive circles was."

She listened in dreamy inattention. "It was a step in the right direction when people began to have afternoon teas. To be sure, there was the biting and chewing sandwiches, but you needn't take them, and most women could manage their teacups gracefully."

"Or hide their faces in them when they couldn't."

"Only," she continued, "the men wouldn't come after the first go off. It was as bad as lunches. Now that the English way of serving tea to callers has come in, it's better. You really get the men, and it keeps them from taking cocktails so much."

"They're rather glad of that. But still, still, there's the guttling and guzzling."

"It's reduced to a minimum."

"But it's there. And the first thing you know you've loaded yourself up with cake or bread-and-butter and spoiled your appetite for dinner. No, afternoon tea must go with the rest of it, if we're going to be truly civilized. If people could come to one another's tables with full minds instead of stomachs, there would be some excuse for hospitality. Perhaps if we reversed the practice of the professional diner-out, and read up at home as he now eats at home, and— No, I don't see how it could be done. But we might take a leaf from the book of people who are not in society. They never ask anybody to meals if they can possibly help it; if some one happens in at meal-times they tell him to pull up a chair—if they have to, or he shows no signs first of going. But even among these people the instinct of hospitality—the feeding form of it—lurks somewhere. In our farm-boarding days—"

"Don't speak of them!" she implored.

"We once went to an evening party," he pursued, "where raw apples and cold water were served."

"I thought I should die of hunger. And when we got home to our own farmer's we ravaged the pantry for everything left from supper. It wasn't much. There!" Lindora screamed. "There is the taxi!" And the shuddering sound of the clock making time at their expense penetrated from the street. "Come!"

"How the instinct of economy lingers in us, too, long after the use of it is outgrown. It's as bad as the instinct of hospitality. We could easily afford to pay extra for the comfort of sitting here over these broken victuals—"

"I tell you we shall be left," she retorted; and in the thirty-five minutes they had at the station before their train started she outlined a scheme of social reform which she meant to put in force as soon as people began to gather in summer force at Lobster Cove.

He derided the notion; but she said, "You will see!" and in rather more time than it takes to tell it they were settled in their cottage, where, after some unavoidable changes of cook and laundress, they were soon in perfect running order.

By this time Lobster Cove was in the full tide of lunching and being lunched. The lunches were almost exclusively ladies' lunches, and the ladies came to them with appetites sharpened by the incomparable air of those real Lobster Cove days which were all cloudless skies and west winds, and by the vigorous automobile exercise of getting to one another's cottages. They seized every pretext for giving these feasts, marked each by some vivid touch of invention within the limits of the graceful convention which all felt bound not to transcend. It was some surprising flavor in the salad, or some touch of color appealing to the eye only; or it was some touch in the ice-cream, or some daring substitution of a native dish for it, as strawberry or peach shortcake; or some bold transposition in the order of the courses; or some capricious arrangement of the decoration, or the use of wild flowers, or even weeds (as meadow-rue or field-lilies), for the local florist's flowers, which set the ladies screaming at the moment and talking of it till the next lunch. This would follow perhaps the next day, or the next but one, according as a new cottager's claims insisted or a lady had a change of guests, or three days at the latest, for no reason.

In their rapid succession people scarcely noticed that Lindora had not given a lunch, and she had so far abandoned herself to the enjoyment of the others' lunches that she had half forgotten her high purposes of reform, when she was sharply recalled to them by a lunch which had not at all agreed with her; she had, in fact, had to have the doctor, and many people had asked one another whether they had heard how she was. Then she took her good resolution in both hands and gave an afternoon, asking people by note or 'phone simply whether they would not come in at four sharp. People were a good deal mystified, but for this very reason everybody came. Some of them came from somebody's lunch, which had been so nice that they lingered over it till four, and then walked, partly to fill in the time and partly to walk off the lunch, as there would be sure to be something at Lindora's later on.

It would be invidious to say what the nature of Lindora's entertainment was. It was certainly to the last degree original, and those who said the worst of it could say no worse than that it was queer. It quite filled the time till six o'clock, and may be perhaps best described as a negative rather than a positive triumph, though what Lindora had aimed at she had undoubtedly achieved. Whatever it was, whether original or queer, it was certainly novel.

A good many men had come, one at least to every five ladies, but as the time passed and a certain blankness began to gather over the spirits of all, they fell into different attitudes of the despair which the ladies did their best to pass off for rapture. At each unscheduled noise they started in a vain expectation, and when the end came, it came so without accent, so without anything but the clock to mark it as the close, that they could hardly get themselves together for going away. They did what was nice and right, of course, in thanking Lindora for her fascinating afternoon, but when they were well beyond hearing one said to another: "Well, I shall certainly have an appetite for my dinner to-night! Why, if there had only been a cup of the weakest kind of tea, or even of cold water!"

Then those who had come in autos gathered as many pedestrians into them as they would hold in leaving the house, or caught them up fainting by the way.

Lindora and Florindo watched them from their veranda.

"Well, my dear," he said, "it's been a wonderful afternoon; an immense stride forward in the cause of anti-eating—or—"

"Don't speak to me!" she cried.

"But it leaves one rather hungry, doesn't it?"

"Hungry!" she hurled back at him. "I could eat a—I don't know what!"

XV
CITY AND COUNTRY IN THE FALL
A Long-distance Eclogue

Morrison. Hello! Hello! Is that you, Wetherbee?

Wetherbee. Yes. Who are you? What do you want with me?

Morrison. Oh, nothing much. It's Morrison, you know;
Morrison—down at Clamhurst Shortsands.

Wetherbee. Oh!
Why, Morrison, of course! Of course, I know!
How are you, Morrison? And, by the way,
Where are you? What! You never mean to say
You are down there yet? Well, by the Holy Poker!
What are you doing there, you ancient joker?

Morrison. Sticking it out over Thanksgiving Day.
I said I would. I tell you, it is gay
Down here. You ought to see the Hunter's Moon,
These silver nights, prinking in our lagoon.
You ought to see our sunsets, glassy red,
Shading to pink and violet overhead.
You ought to see our mornings, still and clear,
White silence, far as you can look and hear.
You ought to see the leaves—our oaks and ashes
Crimson and yellow, with those gorgeous splashes,
Purple and orange, against the bluish green
Of the pine woods; and scattered in between
The scarlet of the maples; and the blaze
Of blackberry-vines, along the dusty ways
And on the old stone walls; the air just balm,
And the crows cawing through the perfect calm
Of afternoons all gold and turquoise. Say,
You ought to have been with wife and me to-day,
A drive we took—it would have made you sick:
The pigeons and the partridges so thick;
And on the hill just beyond Barkin's lane,
Before you reach the barn of Widow Payne,
Showing right up against the sky, as clear
And motionless as sculpture, stood a deer!
Say, does that jar you just a little? Say,
How have you found things up there, anyway,
Since you got back? Air like a cotton string
To breathe? The same old dust on everything,
And in your teeth, and in your eyes? The smoke
From the soft coal, got long beyond a joke?
The trolleys rather more upon your curves,
And all the roar and clatter in your nerves?
Don't you wish you had stayed here, too?

Wetherbee. Well, yes,
I do at certain times, I must confess.
I swear it is enough at times to make you swear
You would almost rather be anywhere
Than here. The building up and pulling down,
The getting to and fro about the town,
The turmoil underfoot and overhead,
Certainly make you wish that you were dead,
At first; and all the mean vulgarity
Of city life, the filth and misery
You see around you, make you want to put
Back to the country anywhere, hot-foot.
Yet—there are compensations.

Morrison. Such as?

Wetherbee. Why,
There is the club.

Morrison. The club I can't deny.
Many o' the fellows back there?

Wetherbee. Nearly all.
Over the twilight cocktails there are tall
Stories and talk. But you would hardly care;
You have the natives to talk with down there,
And always find them meaty.

Morrison. Well, so-so.
Their words outlast their ideas at times, you know,
And they have staying powers. The theaters
All open now?

Wetherbee. Yes, all. And it occurs
To me: there's one among the things that you
Would have enjoyed; an opera with the new—
Or at least the last—music by Sullivan,
And words, though not Gilbertian, that ran
Trippingly with it. Oh, I tell you what,
I'd rather that you had been there than not.

Morrison. Thanks ever so!

Wetherbee. Oh, there is nothing mean
About your early friend. That deer and autumn scene

Were kind of you! And, say, I think you like
Afternoon teas when good. I have chanced to strike
Some of the best of late, where people said
They had sent you cards, but thought you must be dead.
I told them I left you down there by the sea,
And then they sort of looked askance at me,
As if it were a joke, and bade me get
Myself some bouillon or some chocolate,
And turned the subject—did not even give
Me time to prove it is not life to live
In town as long as you can keep from freezing
Beside the autumn sea. A little sneezing,
At Clamhurst Shortsands, since the frosts set in?

Morrison. Well, not enough to make a true friend grin.
Slight colds, mere nothings. With our open fires
We've all the warmth and cheer that heart desires.
Next year we'll have a furnace in, and stay
Not till Thanksgiving, but till Christmas Day.
It's glorious in these roomy autumn nights
To sit between the firelight and the lights
Of our big lamps, and read aloud by turns
As long as kerosene or hickory burns.
We hate to go to bed.

Wetherbee. Of course you do!
And hate to get up in the morning, too—
To pull the coverlet from your frost-bit nose,
And touch the glary matting with your toes!
Are you beginning yet to break the ice
In your wash-pitchers? No? Well, that is nice.
I always hate to do it—seems as if
Summer was going; but when your hand is stiff
With cold, it can be done. Still, I prefer
To wash and dress beside my register,
When summer gets a little on, like this.
But some folks find the other thing pure bliss—
Lusty young chaps, like you.

Morrison. And some folks find
A sizzling radiator to their mind.
What else have you, there, you could recommend
To the attention of a country friend?

Wetherbee. Well, you know how it is in Madison Square,

Late afternoons, now, if the day's been fair—
How all the western sidewalk ebbs and flows
With pretty women in their pretty clo'es:
I've never seen them prettier than this year.
Of course, I know a dear is not a deer,
But still, I think that if I had to meet
One or the other in the road, or street,
All by myself, I am not sure but that
I'd choose the dear that wears the fetching hat.

Morrison. Get out! What else?

Wetherbee. Well, it is not so bad,
If you are feeling a little down, or sad,
To walk along Fifth Avenue to the Park,
When the day thinks perhaps of getting dark,
And meet that mighty flood of vehicles
Laden with all the different kinds of swells,
Homing to dinner, in their carriages—
Victorias, landaus, chariots, coupés—
There's nothing like it to lift up the heart
And make you realize yourself a part,
Sure, of the greatest show on earth.

Morrison. Oh, yes,
I know. I've felt that rapture more or less.
But I would rather put it off as long
As possible. I suppose you like the song
Of the sweet car-gongs better than the cry
Of jays and yellowhammers when the sky
Begins to redden these October mornings,
And the loons sound their melancholy warnings;
Or honk of the wild-geese that write their A
Along the horizon in the evening's gray.
Or when the squirrels look down on you and bark
From the nut trees—

Wetherbee. We have them in the Park
Plenty enough. But, say, you aged sinner,
Have you been out much recently at dinner?

Morrison. What do you mean? You know there's no one here
That dines except ourselves now.

Wetherbee. Well, that's queer!
I thought the natives— But I recollect!

It was not reasonable to expect—

Morrison. What are you driving at?

Wetherbee. Oh, nothing much.
But I was thinking how you come in touch
With life at the first dinner in the fall,
When you get back, first, as you can't at all
Later along. But you, of course, won't care
With your idyllic pleasures.

Morrison. Who was there?

Wetherbee. Oh—ha, ha! What d'you mean by there?

Morrison. Come off!

Wetherbee. What! you remain to pray that came to scoff!

Morrison. You know what I am after.

Wetherbee. Yes, that dinner.
Just a round dozen: Ferguson and Binner
For the fine arts; Bowyer the novelist;
Dr. Le Martin; the psychologist
Fletcher; the English actor Philipson;
The two newspaper Witkins, Bob and John;
A nice Bostonian, Bane the archæologer,
And a queer Russian amateur astrologer;
And Father Gray, the jolly ritualist priest,
And last your humble servant, but not least.
The food was not so filthy, and the wine
Was not so poison. We made out to dine
From eight till one A.M. One could endure
The dinner. But, oh say! The talk was poor!
Your natives down at Clamhurst—

Morrison. Look ye here!
What date does Thanksgiving come on this year?

Wetherbee. Why, I suppose—although I don't remember
Certainly—the usual th November.

Morrison. Novem—You should have waited to get sober!
It comes on the th of October!
And that's to-morrow; and if you happen down

Later, you'd better look for us in town.

XVI
TABLE TALK

They were talking after dinner in that cozy moment when the conversation has ripened, just before the coffee, into mocking guesses and laughing suggestions. The thing they were talking of was something that would have held them apart if less happily timed and placed, but then and there it drew these together in what most of them felt a charming and flattering intimacy. Not all of them took part in the talk, and of those who did, none perhaps assumed to talk with authority or finality. At first they spoke of the subject as it, forbearing to name it, as if the name of it would convey an unpleasant shock, out of temper with the general feeling.

"I don't suppose," the host said, "that it's really so much commoner than it used to be. But the publicity is more invasive and explosive. That's perhaps because it has got higher up in the world and has spread more among the first circles. The time was when you seldom heard of it there, and now it is scarcely a scandal. I remember that when I went abroad, twenty or thirty years ago, and the English brought me to book about it, I could put them down by saying that I didn't know a single divorced person."

"And of course," a bachelor guest ventured, "a person of that sort must be single."

At first the others did not take the joke; then they laughed, but the women not so much as the men.

"And you couldn't say that now?" the lady on the right of the host inquired.

"Why, I don't know," he returned, thoughtfully, after a little interval. "I don't just call one to mind."

"Then," the bachelor said, "that classes you. If you moved in our best society you would certainly know some of the many smart people whose disunions alternate with the morning murders in the daily papers."

"Yes, the fact seems to rank me rather low; but I'm rather proud of the fact."

The hostess seemed not quite to like this arrogant humility. She said, over the length of the table (it was not very long), "I'm sure you know some very nice people who have not been."

"Well, yes, I do. But are they really smart people? They're of very good family, certainly."

"You mustn't brag," the bachelor said.

A husband on the right of the hostess wondered if there were really more of the thing than there used to be.

"Qualitatively, yes, I should say. Quantitatively, I'm not convinced," the host answered. "In a good many of the States it's been made difficult."

The husband on the right of the hostess was not convinced, he said, as to the qualitative increase. The parties to the suits were rich enough, and sometimes they were high enough placed and far enough derived. But there was nearly always a leak in them, a social leak somewhere, on one side or the other. They could not be said to be persons of quality in the highest sense.

"Why, persons of quality seldom can be," the bachelor contended.

The girl opposite, who had been invited to balance him in the scale of celibacy by the hostess in her study of her dinner-party, first smiled, and then alleged a very distinguished instance of divorce in which the parties were both of immaculate origin and unimpeachable fashion. "Nobody," she said, "can accuse them of a want of quality." She was good-looking, though no longer so young as she could have wished; she flung out her answer to the bachelor defiantly, but she addressed it to the host, and he said that was true; certainly it was a signal case; but wasn't it exceptional? The others mentioned like cases, though none quite so perfect, and then there was a lull till the husband on the left of the hostess noted a fact which renewed the life of the discussion.

"There was a good deal of agitation, six or eight years ago, about it. I don't know whether the agitation accomplished anything."

The host believed it had influenced legislation.

"For or against?" the bachelor inquired.

"Oh, against."

"But in other countries it's been coming in more and more. It seems to be as easy in England now as it used to be in Indiana. In France it's nothing scandalous, and in Norwegian society you meet so many disunited couples in a state of quadruplicate reunion that it is very embarrassing. It doesn't seem to bother the parties to the new relation themselves."

"It's very common in Germany, too," the husband on the right of the hostess said.

The husband on her left side said he did not know just how it was in Italy and

Spain, and no one offered to disperse his ignorance.

In the silence which ensued the lady on the left of the host created a diversion in her favor by saying that she had heard they had a very good law in Switzerland.

Being asked to tell what it was, she could not remember, but her husband, on the right of the hostess, saved the credit of his family by supplying her defect. "Oh, yes. It's very curious. We heard of it when we were there. When people want to be put asunder, for any reason or other, they go before a magistrate and declare their wish. Then they go home, and at the end of a certain time— weeks or months—the magistrate summons them before him with a view to reconciliation. If they come, it is a good sign; if they don't come, or come and persist in their desire, then they are summoned after another interval, and are either reconciled or put asunder, as the case may be, or as they choose. It is not expensive, and I believe it isn't scandalous."

"It seems very sensible," the husband on the left of the hostess said, as if to keep the other husband in countenance. But for an interval no one else joined him, and the mature girl said to the man next her that it seemed rather cold-blooded. He was a man who had been entreated to come in, on the frank confession that he was asked as a stop-gap, the original guest having fallen by the way. Such men are apt to abuse their magnanimity, their condescension. They think that being there out of compassion, and in compliance with a hospitality that had not at first contemplated their presence, they can say anything; they are usually asked without but through their wives, who are asked to "lend" them, and who lend them with a grudge veiled in eager acquiescence; and the men think it will afterward advantage them with their wives, when they find they are enjoying themselves, if they will go home and report that they said something vexing or verging on the offensive to their hostess. This man now addressed himself to the lady at the head of the table.

"Why do we all talk as if we thought divorce was an unquestionable evil?"

The hostess looked with a frightened air to the right and left, and then down the table to her husband. But no one came to her rescue, and she asked feebly, as if foreboding trouble (for she knew she had taken a liberty with this man's wife), "Why, don't we?"

"About one in seven of us doesn't," the stop-gap said.

"Oh!" the girl beside him cried out, in a horror-stricken voice which seemed not to interpret her emotion truly. "Is it so bad as that?"

"Perhaps not quite, even if it is bad at all," he returned, and the hostess smiled gratefully at the girl for drawing his fire. But it appeared she had not, for he directed his further speech at the hostess again: really the most inoffensive person there, and the least able to contend with adverse opinions.

"No, I don't believe we do think it an unquestionable evil, unless we think marriage is so." Everybody sat up, as the stop-gap had intended, no doubt, and he "held them with his glittering eye," or as many as he could sweep with his glance. "I suppose that the greatest hypocrite at this table, where we are all so frankly hypocrites together, will not deny that marriage is the prime cause of divorce. In fact, divorce couldn't exist without it."

The women all looked bewilderedly at one another, and then appealingly at the men. None of these answered directly, but the bachelor softly intoned out of Gilbert and Sullivan—he was of that date:

"'A paradox, a paradox;
A most ingenious paradox!'"

"Yes," the stop-gap defiantly assented. "A paradox; and all aboriginal verities, all giant truths, are paradoxes."

"Giant truths is good," the bachelor noted, but the stop-gap did not mind him.

He turned to the host: "I suppose that if divorce is an evil, and we wish to extirpate it, we must strike at its root, at marriage?"

The host laughed. "I prefer not to take the floor. I'm sure we all want to hear what you have to say in support of your mammoth idea."

"Oh yes, indeed," the women chorused, but rather tremulously, as not knowing what might be coming.

"Which do you mean? That all truth is paradoxical, or that marriage is the mother of divorce?"

"Whichever you like."

"The last proposition is self-evident," the stop-gap said, supplying himself with a small bunch of the grapes which nobody ever takes at dinner; the hostess was going to have coffee for the women in the drawing-room, and to leave the men to theirs with their tobacco at the table. "And you must allow that if divorce is a good thing or a bad thing, it equally partakes of the nature of its parent. Or else there's nothing in heredity."

"Oh, come!" one of the husbands said.

"Very well!" the stop-gap submitted. "I yield the word to you." But as the other went no further, he continued. "The case is so clear that it needs no argument. Up to this time, in dealing with the evil of divorce, if it is an evil, we have simply been suppressing the symptoms; and your Swiss method—"

"Oh, it isn't mine," the man said who had stated it.

"—Is only a part of the general practice. It is another attempt to make divorce difficult, when it is marriage that ought to be made difficult."

"Some," the daring bachelor said, "think it ought to be made impossible." The girl across the table began to laugh hysterically, but caught herself up and tried to look as if she had not laughed at all.

"I don't go as far as that," the stop-gap resumed, "but as an inveterate enemy of divorce—"

An "Oh!" varying from surprise to derision chorused up; but he did not mind it; he went on as if uninterrupted.

"I should put every possible obstacle, and at every step, in the way of marriage. The attitude of society toward marriage is now simply preposterous, absolutely grotesque. Society? The whole human framework in all its manifestations, social, literary, religious, artistic, and civic, is perpetually guilty of the greatest mischief in the matter. Nothing is done to retard or prevent marriage; everything to accelerate and promote it. Marriage is universally treated as a virtue which of itself consecrates the lives of the mostly vulgar and entirely selfish young creatures who enter into it. The blind and witless passion in which it oftenest originates, at least with us, is flattered out of all semblance to its sister emotions, and revered as if it were a celestial inspiration, a spiritual impulse. But is it? I defy any one here to say that it is."

As if they were afraid of worse things if they spoke, the company remained silent. But this did not save them.

"You all know it isn't. You all know that it is the caprice of chance encounter, the result of propinquity, the invention of poets and novelists, the superstition of the victims, the unscrupulous make-believe of the witnesses. As an impulse it quickly wears itself out in marriage, and makes way for divorce. In this country nine-tenths of the marriages are love-matches. The old motives which delay and prevent marriage in other countries, aristocratic countries, like questions of rank and descent, even of money, do not exist. Yet this is the land of unhappy unions beyond all other lands, the very home of divorce. The conditions of marriage are ideally favorable according to the opinions of its friends, who are all more or less active in bottling husbands and wives up in its felicity and preventing their escape through divorce."

Still the others were silent, and again the stop-gap triumphed on. "Now, I am an enemy of divorce, too; but I would have it begin before marriage."

"Rather paradoxical again?" the bachelor alone had the hardihood to suggest.

"Not at all. I am quite literal. I would have it begin with the engagement. I would have the betrothed—the mistress and the lover—come before the magistrate or the minister, and declare their motives in wishing to marry, and then I would have him reason with them, and represent that they were acting emotionally in obedience to a passion which must soon spend itself, or a fancy which they would quickly find illusory. If they agreed with him, well and good; if not, he should dismiss them to their homes, for say three months, to think it over. Then he should summon them again, and again reason with them, and dismiss them as before, if they continued obstinate. After three months more, he should call them before him and reason with them for the last time. If they persisted in spite of everything, he should marry them, and let them take the consequences."

The stop-gap leaned back in his chair defiantly, and fixed the host with an eye of challenge. Upon the whole the host seemed not so much frightened. He said: "I don't see anything so original in all that. It's merely a travesty of the Swiss law of divorce."

"And you see nothing novel, nothing that makes for the higher civilization in the application of that law to marriage? You all approve of that law because you believe it prevents nine-tenths of the divorces; but if you had a law that would similarly prevent nine-tenths of the marriages, you would need no divorce law at all."

"Oh, I don't know that," the hardy bachelor said. "What about the one-tenth of the marriages which it didn't prevent? Would you have the parties hopelessly shut up to them? Would you forbid them all hope of escape? Would you have no divorce for any cause whatever?"

"Yes," the husband on the right of the hostess asked (but his wife on the right of the host looked as if she wished he had not mixed in), "wouldn't more unhappiness result from that one marriage than from all the marriages as we have them now?"

"Aren't you both rather precipitate?" the stop-gap demanded. "I said, let the parties to the final marriage take the consequences. But if these consequences were too dire, I would not forbid them the hope of relief. I haven't thought the matter out very clearly yet, but there are one or two causes for divorce which I would admit."

"Ah?" the host inquired, with a provisional smile.

"Yes, causes going down into the very nature of things—the nature of men and of women. Incompatibility of temperament ought always to be very seriously considered as a cause."

"Yes?"

"And, above all," and here the stop-gap swept the board with his eye, "difference of sex."

The sort of laugh which expresses uncertainty of perception and conditional approval went up.

The hostess rose with rather a frightened air. "Shall we leave them to their tobacco?" she said to the other women.

When he went home the stop-gap celebrated his triumph to his wife. "I don't think she'll ask you for the loan of me again to fill a place without you."

"Yes," she answered, remotely. "You don't suppose she'll think we live unhappily together?"

XVII
THE ESCAPADE OF A GRANDFATHER

"Well, what are you doing here?" the younger of the two sages asked, with a resolute air of bonhomie, as he dragged himself over the asphalt path, and sank, gasping, into the seat beside the other in the Park. His senior lifted his head and looked him carefully over to make sure of his identity, and then he said:

"I suppose, to answer your fatuous question, I am waiting here to get my breath before I move on; and in the next place, I am watching the feet of the women who go by in their high-heeled shoes."

"How long do you think it will take you to get your breath in the atmosphere of these motors?" the younger sage pursued. "And you don't imagine that these women are of the first fashion, do you?"

"No, but I imagine their shoes are. I have been calculating that their average heel is from an inch and a half to two inches high, and touches the ground in the circumference of a twenty-five-cent piece. As you seem to be fond of asking questions, perhaps you will like to answer one. Why do you think they do it?"

"Wear shoes like that?" the younger returned, cheerily, and laughed as he added, "Because the rest do."

"Mmm!" the elder grumbled, not wholly pleased, and yet not refusing the answer. He had been having a little touch of grippe, and was somewhat broken from his wonted cynicism. He said: "It's very strange, very sad. Just now there was such a pretty young girl, so sweet and fine, went tottering by as helpless, in any exigency, as the daughter of a thousand years of bound-feet Chinese women. While she tilted on, the nice young fellow with her swept forward with one stride to her three on the wide soles and low heels of nature-last boots, and kept himself from out-walking her by a devotion that made him grit his teeth. Probably she was wiser and better and brighter than he, but she didn't look it; and I, who voted to give her the vote the other day, had my misgivings. I think I shall satisfy myself for the next five years by catching cold in taking my hat off to her in elevators, and getting killed by automobiles in helping her off the cars, where I've given her my seat."

"But you must allow that if her shoes are too tight, her skirts are not so tight as they were. Or have you begun sighing for the good old hobble-skirts, now they're gone?"

"The hobble-skirts were prettier than I thought they were when they were with us, but the 'tempestuous petticoat' has its charm, which I find I'd been missing."

"Well, at least it's a change," the younger sage allowed, "and I haven't found the other changes in our dear old New York which I look for when I come back in the fall."

The sages were enjoying together the soft weather which lingered with us a whole month from the middle of October onward, and the afternoon of their meeting in the Park was now softly reddening to the dim sunset over the westward trees.

"Yes," the elder assented. "I miss the new sky-scrapers which used to welcome me back up and down the Avenue. But there are more automobiles than ever, and the game of saving your life from them when you cross the street is madder and merrier than I have known it before."

"The war seems to have stopped building because people can't afford it," the other suggested, "but it has only increased automobiling."

"Well, people can't afford that, either. Nine-tenths of them are traveling the road to ruin, I'm told, and apparently they can't get over the ground too fast. Just look!" and the sages joined in the amused and mournful contemplation of the different types of motors innumerably whirring up and down the drive before them, while they choked in the fumes of the gasolene.

The motors were not the costliest types, except in a few instances, and in most instances they were the cheaper types, such as those who could not afford them could at least afford best. The sages had found a bench beside the walk where the statue of Daniel Webster looks down on the confluence of two driveways, and the stream of motors, going and coming, is like a seething torrent either way.

"The mystery is," the elder continued, "why they should want to do it in the way they do it. Are they merely going somewhere and must get there in the shortest time possible, or are they arriving on a wager? If they are taking a pleasure drive, what a droll idea of pleasure they must have! Maybe they are trying to escape Black Care, but they must know he sits beside the chauffeur as he used to sit behind the horseman, and they know that he has a mortgage in his pocket, and can foreclose it any time on the house they have hypothecated to buy their car. Ah!" The old man started forward with the involuntary impulse of rescue. But it was not one of the people who singly, or in terrorized groups, had been waiting at the roadside to find their way across; it was only a hapless squirrel of those which used to make their way safely among the hoofs and wheels of the kind old cabs and carriages, and it lay instantly crushed under the tire of a motor. "He's done for, poor little wretch! They can't get used to the change. Some day a policeman will pick me up from under a second-hand motor. I wonder what the great Daniel from his pedestal up there would say if he came to judgment."

"He wouldn't believe in the change any more than that squirrel. He would decide that he was dreaming, and would sleep on, forgetting and forgotten."

"Forgotten," the elder sage assented. "I remember when his fame filled the United States, which was then the whole world to me. And now I don't imagine that our hyphenated citizens have the remotest consciousness of him. If Daniel began delivering one of his liberty-and-union-now-and-forever-one-and-inseparable speeches, they wouldn't know what he was talking about." The sage laughed and champed his toothless jaws together, as old men do in the effort to compose their countenances after an emotional outbreak.

"Well, for one thing," the younger observed, "they wouldn't understand what he said. You will notice, if you listen to them going by, that they seldom speak English. That's getting to be a dead language in New York, though it's still used in the newspapers." He thought to hearten the other with his whimsicality, for it seemed to him that the elder sage was getting sensibly older since their last meeting, and that he would be the gayer for such cheer as a man on the hither side of eighty can offer a man on the thither. "Perhaps the Russian Jews would appreciate Daniel if he were put into Yiddish for them. They're the brightest intelligences among our hyphenates. And they have the old-fashioned ideals of liberty and humanity, perhaps because they've known so little of either."

His gaiety did not seem to enliven his senior much. "Ah, the old ideals!" he sighed. "The old ideal of an afternoon airing was a gentle course in an open carriage on a soft drive. Now it's a vertiginous whirl on an asphalted road, round and round and round the Park till the victims stagger with their brains spinning after they get out of their cars."

The younger sage laughed. "You've been listening to the pessimism of the dear old fellows who drive the few lingering victorias. If you'd believe them, all these people in the motors are chauffeurs giving their lady-friends joy-rides."

"Few?" the elder retorted. "There are lots of them. I've counted twenty in a single round of the Park. I was proud to be in one of them, though my horse left something to be desired in the way of youth and beauty. But I reflected that I was not very young or beautiful myself."

As the sages sat looking out over the dizzying whirl of the motors they smoothed the tops of their sticks with their soft old hands, and were silent oftener than not. The elder seemed to drowse off from the time and place, but he was recalled by the younger saying, "It is certainly astonishing weather for this season of the year."

The elder woke up and retorted, as if in offense: "Not at all. I've seen the cherries in blossom at the end of October."

"They didn't set their fruit, I suppose."

"Well—no."

"Ah! Well, I saw a butterfly up here in the sheep-pasture the other day. I could have put out my hand and caught it. It's the soft weather that brings your victorias out like the belated butterflies. Wait till the first cold snap, and there won't be a single victoria or butterfly left."

"Yes," the elder assented, "we butterflies and victorias belong to the youth of the year and the world. And the sad thing is that we won't have our palingenesis."

"Why not?" the younger sage demanded. "What is to prevent your coming back in two or three thousand years?"

"Well, if we came back in a year even, we shouldn't find room, for one reason. Haven't you noticed how full to bursting the place seems? Every street is as packed as lower Fifth Avenue used to be when the operatives came out of the big shops for their nooning. The city's shell hasn't been enlarged or added to, but the life in it has multiplied past its utmost capacity. All the hotels and houses and flats are packed. The theaters, wherever the plays are bad enough, swarm with spectators. Along up and down every side-streets the motors stand in rows, and at the same time the avenues are so dense with them that you are killed at every crossing. There has been no building to speak of during the summer, but unless New York is overbuilt next year we must appeal to Chicago to come and help hold it. But I've an idea that the victorias are remaining to stay; if some sort of mechanical horse could be substituted for the poor old animals that remind me of my mortality, I should be sure of it. Every now and then I get an impression of permanence in the things of the Park. As long as the peanut-men and the swan-boats are with us I sha'n't quite despair. And the other night I was moved almost to tears by the sight of a four-in-hand tooling softly down the Fifth Avenue drive. There it was, like some vehicular phantom, but how, whence, when? It came, as if out of the early eighteen-nineties; two middle-aged grooms, with their arms folded, sat on the rumble (if it's the rumble), but of all the young people who ought to have flowered over the top none was left but the lady beside the gentleman-driver on the box. I've tried every evening since for that four-in-hand, but I haven't seen it, and I've decided it wasn't a vehicular phantom, but a mere dream of the past."

"Four-horse dream," the younger sage commented, as if musing aloud.

The elder did not seem quite pleased. "A joke?" he challenged.

"Not necessarily. I suppose I was the helpless prey of the rhyme."

"I didn't know you were a poet."

"I'm not, always. But didn't it occur to you that danger for danger your four-in-hand was more dangerous than an automobile to the passing human creature?"

"It might have been if it had been multiplied by ten thousand. But there was only one of it, and it wasn't going twenty miles an hour."

"That's true," the younger sage assented. "But there was always a fearful hazard in horses when we had them. We supposed they were tamed, but, after all, they were only trained animals, like Hagenback's."

"And what is a chauffeur?"

"Ah, you have me there!" the younger said, and he laughed generously. "Or you would have if I hadn't noticed something like amelioration in the chauffeurs. At any rate, the taxis are cheaper than they were, and I suppose something will be done about the street traffic some time. They're talking now about subway crossings. But I should prefer overhead foot-bridges at all the corners, crossing one another diagonally. They would look like triumphal arches, and would serve the purpose of any future Dewey victory if we should happen to have another hero to win one."

"Well, we must hope for the best. I rather like the notion of the diagonal foot-bridges. But why not Rows along the second stories as they have them in Chester? I should be pretty sure of always getting home alive if we had them. Now if I'm not telephoned for at a hospital before I'm restored to consciousness, I think myself pretty lucky. And yet it seems but yesterday, as the people used to say in the plays, since I had a pride in counting the automobiles as I walked up the Avenue. Once I got as high as twenty before I reached Fifty-ninth Street. Now I couldn't count as many horse vehicles."

The elder sage mocked himself in a feeble laugh, but the younger tried to be serious. "We don't realize the absolute change. Our streets are not streets any more; they are railroad tracks with locomotives let loose on them, and no signs up to warn people at the crossings. It's pathetic to see the foot-passengers saving themselves, especially the poor, pretty, high-heeled women, looking this way and that in their fright, and then tottering over as fast as they can totter."

"Well, I should have said it was outrageous, humiliating, insulting, once, but I don't any more; it would be no use."

"No; and so much depends upon the point of view. When I'm on foot I feel all my rights invaded, but when I'm in a taxi it amuses me to see the women escaping; and I boil with rage in being halted at every other corner by the policeman with his new-fangled semaphore, and it's "Go" and "Stop" in red and blue, and my taxi-clock going round all the time and getting me in for a dollar when I thought I should keep within seventy cents. Then I feel that pedestrians of every age and sex ought to be killed."

"Yes, there's something always in the point of view; and there's some comfort when you're stopped in your taxi to feel that they often do get killed."

The sages laughed together, and the younger said: "I suppose when we get aeroplanes in common use, there'll be annoying traffic regulations, and policemen anchored out at intervals in the central blue to enforce them. After all—"

What he was going to add in amplification cannot be known, for a girlish voice, trying to sharpen itself from its native sweetness to a conscientious severity, called to them as its owner swiftly advanced upon the elder sage: "Now, see here, grandfather! This won't do at all. You promised not to leave that bench by the Indian Hunter, and here you are away down by the Falconer, and we've been looking everywhere for you. It's too bad! I shall be afraid to trust you at all after this. Why, it's horrid of you, grandfather! You might have got killed crossing the drive."

The grandfather looked up and verified the situation, which seemed to include a young man, tall and beautiful, but neither so handsome nor so many heads high as the young men in the advertisements of ready-to-wear clothing, who smiled down on the young girl as if he had arrived with her, and were finding an amusement in her severity which he might not, later. She was, in fact, very pretty, and her skirt flared in the fashion of the last moment, as she stooped threateningly yet fondly over her grandfather.

The younger sage silently and somewhat guiltily escaped from the tumult of emotion which ignored him, and shuffled slowly down the path. The other finally gave an "Oh!" of recognition, and then said, for all explanation and excuse, "I didn't know what had become of you," and then they all laughed.

XVIII
SELF-SACRIFICE: A FARCE-TRAGEDY
I

Miss Ramsey: "And they were really understood to be engaged?" Miss Ramsey is a dark-eyed, dark-haired girl of nearly the length of two lady's umbrellas and the bulk of one closely folded in its sheath. She stands with her elbow supported on the corner of the mantel, her temple resting on the knuckle of a thin, nervous hand, in an effect of thoughtful absent-mindedness. Miss Garnett, more or less Merovingian in a costume that lends itself somewhat reluctantly to a low, thick figure, is apparently poising for departure, as she stands before the chair from which she has risen beside Miss Ramsey's tea-table and looks earnestly up into Miss Ramsey's absent face. Both are very young, but aim at being much older than they are, with occasional lapses into extreme girlhood.

Miss Garnett: "Yes, distinctly. I knew you couldn't know, and I thought you ought to." She speaks in a deep conviction-bearing and conviction-carrying voice. "If he has been coming here so much."

Miss Ramsey, with what seems temperamental abruptness: "Sit down. One can always think better sitting down." She catches a chair under her with a deft movement of her heel, and Miss Garnett sinks provisionally into her seat. "And I think it needs thought, don't you?"

Miss Garnett: "That is what I expected of you."

Miss Ramsey: "And have some more tea. There is nothing like fresh tea for clearing the brain, and we certainly need clear brains for this." She pushes a button in the wall beside her, and is silent till the maid appears. "More tea,

Nora." She is silent again while the maid reappears with the tea and disappears. "I don't know that he has been coming here so very much. But he has no right to be coming at all, if he is engaged. That is, in that way."

Miss Garnett: "No. Not unless—he wishes he wasn't."

Miss Ramsey: "That would give him less than no right."

Miss Garnett: "That is true. I didn't think of it in that light."

Miss Ramsey: "I'm trying to decide what I ought to do if he does want to get off. She said herself that they were engaged?"

Miss Garnett: "As much as that. Conny understood her to say so. And Conny never makes a mistake in what people say. Emily didn't say whom she was engaged to, but Conny felt that that was to come later, and she did not quite feel like asking, don't you know."

Miss Ramsey: "Of course. And how came she to decide that it was Mr. Ashley?"

Miss Garnett: "Simply by putting two and two together. They two were together the whole time last summer."

Miss Ramsey: "I see. Then there is only one thing for me to do."

Miss Garnett, admiringly: "I knew you would say that."

Miss Ramsey, dreamily: "The question is what the thing is."

Miss Garnett: "Yes!"

Miss Ramsey: "That is what I wish to think over. Chocolates?" She offers a box, catching it with her left hand from the mantel at her shoulder, without rising.

Miss Garnett: "Thank you; do you think they go well with tea?"

Miss Ramsey: "They go well with anything. But we mustn't allow our minds to be distracted. The case is simply this: If Mr. Ashley is engaged to Emily Fray, he has no right to go round calling on other girls—well, as if he wasn't—and he has been calling here a great deal. That is perfectly evident. He must be made to feel that girls are not to be trifled with—that they are not mere toys."

Miss Garnett: "How splendidly you do reason! And he ought to understand that Emily has a right—"

Miss Ramsey: "Oh, I don't know that I care about her—or not primarily. Or do you say primarily?"

Miss Garnett: "I never know. I only use it in writing."

Miss Ramsey: "It's a clumsy word; I don't know that I shall. But what I mean is that I must act from a general principle, and that principle is that when a man is engaged, it doesn't matter whether the girl has thrown herself at him, or not—"

Miss Garnett: "She certainly did, from what Conny says."

Miss Ramsey: "He must be shown that other girls won't tolerate his behaving as if he were not engaged. It is wrong."

Miss Garnett: "We must stand together."

Miss Ramsey: "Yes. Though I don't infer that he has been attentive to other girls generally."

Miss Garnett: "No. I meant that if he has been coming here so much, you want to prevent his trifling with others."

Miss Ramsey: "Something like that. But it ought to be more definite. He ought to realize that if another girl cared for him, it would be cruel to her, paying her attentions, when he was engaged to some one else."

Miss Garnett: "And cruel to the girl he is engaged to."

Miss Ramsey: "Yes." She speaks coldly, vaguely. "But that is the personal ground, and I wish to avoid that. I wish to deal with him purely in the abstract."

Miss Garnett: "Yes, I understand that. And at the same time you wish to punish him. He ought to be made to feel it all the more because he is so severe himself."

Miss Ramsey: "Severe?"

Miss Garnett: "Not tolerating anything that's the least out of the way in other people. Taking you up about your ideas and showing where you're wrong, or even silly. Spiritually snubbing, Conny calls it."

Miss Ramsey: "Oh, I like that in him. It's so invigorating. It braces up all your good resolutions. It makes you ashamed; and shame is sanative."

Miss Garnett: "That's just what I told Conny, or the same thing. Do you think another one would hurt me? I will risk it, anyway." She takes another chocolate from the box. "Go on."

Miss Ramsey: "Oh, I was just wishing that I had been out longer, and had a little more experience of men. Then I should know how to act. How do you suppose people do, generally?"

Miss Garnett: "Why, you know, if they find a man in love with them, after he's engaged to another girl, they make him go back to her, it doesn't matter whether they're in love with him themselves or not."

Miss Ramsey: "I'm not in love with Mr. Ashley, please."

Miss Garnett: "No; I'm supposing an extreme case."

Miss Ramsey, after a moment of silent thought: "Did you ever hear of anybody doing it?"

Miss Garnett: "Not just in our set. But I know it's done continually."

Miss Ramsey: "It seems to me as if I had read something of the kind."

Miss Garnett: "Oh yes, the books are full of it. Are those mallows? They might carry off the effects of the chocolates." Miss Ramsey passes her the box of marshmallows which she has bent over the table to look at.

Miss Ramsey: "And of course they couldn't get into the books if they hadn't really happened. I wish I could think of a case in point."

Miss Garnett: "Why, there was Peg Woffington—"

Miss Ramsey, with displeasure: "She was an actress of some sort, wasn't she?"

Miss Garnett, with meritorious candor: "Yes, she was. But she was a very good actress."

Miss Ramsey: "What did she do?"

Miss Garnett: "Well, it's a long time since I read it; and it's rather old-fashioned now. But there was a countryman of some sort, I remember, who came away from his wife, and fell in love with Peg Woffington, and then the wife follows him up to London, and begs her to give him back to her, and she does it. There's something about a portrait of Peg—I don't remember exactly; she puts her face through and cries when the wife talks to the picture. The wife thinks it is a real picture, and she is kind of soliloquizing, and asking Peg to give her husband back to her; and Peg does, in the end. That part is beautiful. They become the greatest friends."

Miss Ramsey: "Rather silly, I should say."

Miss Garnett: "Yes, it is rather silly, but I suppose the author thought she had to do something."

Miss Ramsey: "And disgusting. A married man, that way! I don't see any comparison with Mr. Ashley."

Miss Garnett: "No, there really isn't any. Emily has never asked you to give him up. And besides, Peg Woffington really liked him a little—loved him, in fact."

Miss Ramsey: "And I don't like Mr. Ashley at all. Of course I respect him—and I admire his intellect; there's no question about his being handsome; but I have never thought of him for a moment in any other way; and now I can't even respect him."

Miss Garnett: "Nobody could. I'm sure Emily would be welcome to him as far as I was concerned. But he has never been about with me so much as he has with you, and I don't wonder you feel indignant."

Miss Ramsey, coldly: "I don't feel indignant. I wish to be just."

Miss Garnett: "Yes, that is what I mean. And poor Emily is so uninteresting! In the play that Kentucky Summers does, she is perfectly fascinating at first, and you can see why the poor girl's fiancé should be so taken with her. But I'm sure no one could say you had ever given Mr. Ashley the least encouragement. It would be pure justice on your part. I think you are grand! I shall always be proud of knowing what you were going to do."

Miss Ramsey, after some moments of snubbing intention: "I don't know what I am going to do myself, yet. Or how. What was that play? I never heard of it."

Miss Garnett: "I don't remember distinctly, but it was about a young man who falls in love with her, when he's engaged to another girl, and she determines, as soon as she finds it out, to disgust him, so that he will go back to the other girl, don't you know."

Miss Ramsey: "That sounds rather more practical than the Peg Woffington plan. What does she do?"

Miss Garnett: "Nothing you'd like to do."

Miss Ramsey: "I'd like to do something in such a cause. What does she do?"

Miss Garnett: "Oh, when he is calling on her, Kentucky Summers pretends to fly into a rage with her sister, and she pulls her hair down, and slams everything round the room, and scolds, and drinks champagne, and wants him to drink with her, and I don't know what all. The upshot is that he is only too glad to get away."

Miss Ramsey: "It's rather loathsome, isn't it?"

Miss Garnett: "It is rather loathsome. But it was in a good cause, and I suppose it was what an actress would think of."

Miss Ramsey: "An actress?"

Miss Garnett: "I forgot. The heroine is a distinguished actress, you know, and Kentucky could play that sort of part to perfection. But I don't think a lady would like to cut up, much, in the best cause."

Miss Ramsey: "Cut up?"

Miss Garnett: "She certainly frisks about the room a good deal. How delicious these mallows are! Have you ever tried toasting them?"

Miss Ramsey: "At school. There seems an idea in it. And the hero isn't married. I don't like the notion of a married man."

Miss Garnett: "Oh, I'm quite sure he isn't married. He's merely engaged. That makes the whole difference from the Peg Woffington story. And there's no portrait, I'm confident, so that you wouldn't have to do that part."

Miss Ramsey, haughtily: "I don't propose to do any part, if the affair can't be arranged without some such mountebank business!"

Miss Garnett: "You can manage it, if anybody can. You have so much dignity that you could awe him into doing his duty by a single glance. I wouldn't be in his place!"

Miss Ramsey: "I shall not give him a glance. I shall not see him when he comes. That will be simpler still." To Nora, at the door: "What is it, Nora?"

II

NORA, MISS RAMSEY, MISS GARNETT

Nora: "Mr. Ashley, Miss Ramsey."

Miss Ramsey, with a severity not meant for Nora: "Ask him to sit down in the reception-room a moment."

Nora: "Yes, Miss Ramsey."

III

MISS RAMSEY, MISS GARNETT

Miss Garnett, rising and seizing Miss Ramsey's hands: "Oh, Isobel! But you will be equal to it! Oh! Oh!"

Miss Ramsey, with state: "Why are you going, Esther? Sit down."

Miss Garnett: "If I only could stay! If I could hide under the sofa, or behind the screen! Isn't it wonderful—providential—his coming at the very instant? Oh, Isobel!" She clasps her friend convulsively, and after a moment's resistance Miss Ramsey yields to her emotion, and they hide their faces in each other's neck, and strangle their hysteric laughter. They try to regain their composure, and then abandon the effort with a shuddering delight in the perfection of the incident. "What shall you do? Shall you trust to inspiration? Shall you make him show his hand first, and then act? Or shall you tell him at once that you know all, and— Or no, of course you can't do that. He's not supposed to know that you know. Oh, I can imagine the freezing hauteur that you'll receive him with, and the icy indifference you'll let him understand that he isn't a persona grata with! If I were only as tall as you! He isn't as tall himself, and you can tower over him. Don't sit down, or bend, or anything; just stand with your head up, and glance carelessly at him under your lashes as if nobody was there! Then it will gradually dawn upon him that you know everything, and he'll simply go through the floor." They take some ecstatic turns about the room, Miss Ramsey waltzing as gentleman. She abruptly frees herself.

Miss Ramsey: "No. It can't be as tacit as all that. There must be something explicit. As you say, I must do something to cure him of his fancy—his perfidy—and make him glad to go back to her."

Miss Garnett: "Yes! Do you think he deserves it?"

Miss Ramsey: "I've no wish to punish him."

Miss Garnett: "How noble you are! I don't wonder he adores you. I should. But you won't find it so easy. You must do something drastic. It is drastic, isn't it? or do I mean static? One of those things when you simply crush a person. But now I must go. How I should like to listen at the door! We must kiss each other very quietly, and I must slip out— Oh, you dear! How I long to know what you'll do! But it will be perfect, whatever it is. You always did do perfect things." They knit their fingers together in parting. "On second thoughts I won't kiss you. It might unman you, and you need all your strength. Unman isn't the word, exactly, but you can't say ungirl, can you? It would be ridiculous. Though girls are as brave as men when it comes to duty. Good-by, dear!" She catches Miss Ramsey about the neck, and pressing her lips silently to her cheek, runs out. Miss Ramsey rings and the maid appears.

IV

NORA, MISS RAMSEY

Miss Ramsey, starting: "Oh! Is that you, Nora? Of course! Nora!"

Nora: "Yes, Miss Ramsey."

Miss Ramsey: "Do you know where my brother keeps his cigarettes?"

Nora: "Why, in his room, Miss Ramsey; you told him you didn't like the smell here."

Miss Ramsey: "Yes, yes. I forgot. And has he got any cocktails?"

Nora: "He's got the whole bottle full of them yet."

Miss Ramsey: "Full yet?"

Nora: "You wouldn't let him offer them to the gentlemen he had to lunch, last week, because you said—"

Miss Ramsey: "What did I say?"

Nora: "They were vulgar."

Miss Ramsey: "And so they are. And so much the better! Bring the cigarettes and the bottle and some glasses here, Nora, and then ask Mr. Ashley to come." She walks away to the window, and hurriedly hums a musical comedy waltz, not quite in tune, as from not remembering exactly, and after Nora has tinkled in with a tray of glasses she lights a cigarette and stands puffing it, gasping and coughing a little, as Walter Ashley enters. "Oh, Mr. Ashley! Sorry to make you wait."

V

MR. ASHLEY, MISS RAMSEY

Mr. Ashley: "The time has seemed long, but I could have waited all day. I couldn't have gone without seeing you, and telling you—" He pauses, as if bewildered at the spectacle of Miss Ramsey's resolute practice with the cigarette, which she now takes from her lips and waves before her face with innocent recklessness.

Miss Ramsey, chokingly: "Do sit down." She drops into an easy-chair beside the tea-table, and stretches the tips of her feet out beyond the hem of her skirt in extremely lady-like abandon. "Have a cigarette." She reaches the box to him.

Ashley: "Thank you. I won't smoke, I believe." He stands frowning, while she throws her cigarette into a teacup and lights another.

Miss Ramsey: "I thought everybody smoked. Then have a cocktail."

Ashley: "A what?"

Miss Ramsey: "A cocktail. So many people like them with their tea, instead of rum, you know."

Ashley: "No, I didn't know." He regards her with amaze, rapidly hardening into condemnation.

Miss Ramsey: "I hope you don't object to smoking. Englishwomen all smoke."

Ashley: "I think I've heard. I didn't know that American ladies did."

Miss Ramsey: "They don't, all. But they will when they find how nice it is."

Ashley: "And do Englishwomen all drink cocktails?"

Miss Ramsey: "They will when they find how nice it is. But why do you keep standing? Sit down, if it's only for a moment. There is something I would like to talk with you about. What were you saying when you came in? I didn't catch it quite."

Ashley: "Nothing—now—"

Miss Ramsey: "And I can't persuade you to have a cocktail? I believe I'll have another myself." She takes up the bottle, and tries several times to pour from it. "I do believe Nora's forgotten to open it! That is a good joke on me. But I mustn't let her know. Do you happen to have a pocket-corkscrew with you, Mr. Ashley?"

Ashley: "No—"

Miss Ramsey: "Well, never mind." She tosses her cigarette into the grate, and lights another. "I wonder why they always have cynical persons smoke, on the stage? I don't see that the two things necessarily go together, but it does give you a kind of thrill when they strike a match, and it lights up their faces when they put it to the cigarette. You know something good and wicked is going to happen." She puffs violently at her cigarette, and then suddenly flings it away and starts to her feet. "Will you—would you—open the window?" She collapses into her chair.

Ashley, springing toward her: "Miss Ramsey, are you—you are ill!"

Miss Ramsey: "No, no! The window! A little faint—it's so close— There, it's all right now. Or it will be—when—I've had—another cigarette." She leans forward to take one; Ashley gravely watches her, but says nothing. She lights her cigarette, but, without smoking, throws it away. "Go on."

Ashley: "I wasn't saying anything!"

Miss Ramsey: "Oh, I forgot. And I don't know what we were talking about myself." She falls limply back into her chair and closes her eyes.

Ashley: "Sha'n't I ring for the maid? I'm afraid—"

Miss Ramsey, imperiously: "Not at all. Not on any account." Far less imperiously: "You may pour me a cup of tea if you like. That will make me well. The full strength, please." She motions away the hot-water jug with which he has proposed qualifying the cup of tea which he offers her.

Ashley: "One lump or two?"

Miss Ramsey: "Only one, thank you." She takes the cup.

Ashley, offering the milk: "Cream?"

Miss Ramsey: "A drop." He stands anxiously beside her while she takes a long draught and then gives back the cup. "That was perfect."

Ashley: "Another?"

Miss Ramsey: "No, that is just right. Now go on. Or, I forgot. You were not going on. Oh dear! How much better I feel. There must have been something poisonous in those cigarettes."

Ashley: "Yes, there was tobacco."

Miss Ramsey: "Oh, do you think it was the tobacco? Do throw the whole box into the fire! I shall tell Bob never to get cigarettes with tobacco in them after this. Won't you have one of the chocolates? Or a mallow? I feel as if I should never want to eat anything again. Where was I?" She rests her cheek against the side of her chair cushion, and speaks with closed eyes, in a weak murmur. Mr. Ashley watches her at first with anxiety, then with a gradual change of countenance until a gleam of intelligence steals into his look of compassion.

Ashley: "You asked me to throw the cigarettes into the fire. But I want you to let me keep them."

Miss Ramsey, with wide-flung eyes: "You? You said you wouldn't smoke."

Ashley, laughing: "May I change my mind? One talks better." He lights a cigarette. "And, Miss Ramsey, I believe I will have a cocktail, after all."

Miss Ramsey: "Mr. Ashley!"

Ashley, without noting her protest: "I had forgotten that I had a corkscrew in my pocket-knife. Don't trouble yourself to ring for one." He produces the knife and opens the bottle; then, as Miss Ramsey rises and stands aghast, he pours out a glass and offers it to her, with mock devotion. As she shakes her head and recoils: "Oh! I thought you liked cocktails. They are very good after cigarettes—very reviving. But if you won't—" He tosses off the cocktail and sets down the glass, smacking his lips. "Tell your brother I commend his taste —in cocktails and"—puffing his cigarette—"tobacco. Poison for poison, let me offer you one of my cigarettes. They're milder than these." He puts his hand to his breast pocket.

Miss Ramsey, with nervous shrinking: "No—"

Ashley: "It's just as well. I find that I hadn't brought mine with me." After a moment: "You are so unconventional, so fearless, that I should like your notion of the problem in a book I've just been reading. Why should the mere fact that a man is married to one woman prevent his being in love with another, or half a dozen others; or vice versa?"

Miss Ramsey: "Mr. Ashley, do you wish to insult me?"

Ashley: "Dear me, no! But put the case a little differently. Suppose a couple are merely engaged. Does that fact imply that neither has a right to a change of mind, or to be fancy free to make another choice?"

Miss Ramsey, indignantly: "Yes, it does. They are as sacredly bound to each other as if they were married, and if they are false to each other the girl is a wretch, and the man is a villain! And if you think anything I have said can excuse you for breaking your engagement, or that I don't consider you the wickedest person in the world, and the most barefaced hypocrite, and—and—I don't know what—you are very much mistaken."

Ashley: "What in the world are you talking about?"

Miss Ramsey: "I am talking about you and your shameless perfidy."

Ashley: "My shameless perf— I don't understand! I came here to tell you that I love you—"

Miss Ramsey: "How dare you! To speak to me of that, when— Or perhaps you have broken with her, and think you are free to hoodwink some other poor creature. But you will find that you have chosen the wrong person. And it's no excuse for you her being a little—a little—not so bright as some girls, and not so good-looking. Oh, it's enough to make any girl loathe her own looks! You mustn't suppose you can come here red-handed—yes, it's the same as a murder, and any true girl would say so—and tell me you care for me. No, Walter Ashley, I haven't fallen so low as that, though I have the disgrace of your acquaintance. And I hope—I hope—if you don't like my smoking, and offering you cocktails, and talking the way I have, it will be a lesson to you. And yes!—I will say it! If it will add to your misery to know that I did respect you very much, and thought everything—very highly—of you, and might have answered you very differently before, when you were free to tell me that— now I have nothing but the utmost abhorrence—and—disapproval of you. And —and— Oh, I don't see how you can be so hateful!" She hides her face in her hands and rushes from the room, overturning several chairs in her course toward the door. Ashley remains staring after her, while a succession of impetuous rings make themselves heard from the street door. There is a sound of opening it, and then a flutter of skirts and anxieties, and Miss Garnett comes running into the room.

VI

MISS GARNETT, MR. ASHLEY

Miss Garnett, to the maid hovering in the doorway: "Yes, I must have left it here, for I never missed it till I went to pay my fare in the motor-bus, and tried to think whether I had the exact dime, and if I hadn't whether the conductor would change a five-dollar bill or not, and then it rushed into my mind that I had left my purse somewhere, and I knew I hadn't been anywhere else." She runs from the mantel to the writing-desk in the corner, and then to the sofa, where, peering under the tea-table, she finds her purse on the shelf. "Oh, here it is, Nora, just where I put it when we began to talk, and I must have gone out and left it. I—" She starts with a little shriek, in encountering Ashley. "Oh, Mr. Ashley! What a fright you gave me! I was just looking for my purse that I missed when I went to pay my fare in the motor-bus, and was wondering whether I had the exact dime, or the conductor could change a five-dollar bill, and—" She discovers, or affects to discover, something strange in his manner. "What—what is the matter, Mr. Ashley?"

Ashley: "I shall be glad to have you tell me—or any one."

Miss Garnett: "I don't understand. Has Isobel—"

Ashley: "Miss Garnett, did you know I was engaged?"

Miss Garnett: "Why, yes; I was just going to congrat—"

Ashley: "Well, don't, unless you can tell me whom I am engaged to."

Miss Garnett: "Why, aren't you engaged to Emily Fray?"

Ashley: "Not the least in the world."

Miss Garnett, in despair: "Then what have I done? Oh, what a fatal, fatal scrape!" With a ray of returning hope: "But she told me herself that she was engaged! And you were together so much, last summer!" Desperately: "Then if she isn't engaged to you, whom is she engaged to?"

Ashley: "On general principles, I shouldn't know, but in this particular instance I happen to know that she is engaged to Owen Brooks. They were a great deal more together last summer."

Miss Garnett, with conviction: "So they were!" With returning doubt: "But why didn't she say so?"

Ashley: "I can't tell you; she may have had her reasons, or she may not. Can you possibly tell me, in return for my ignorance, why the fact of her engagement should involve me in the strange way it seems to have done with Miss Ramsey?"

Miss Garnett, with a burst of involuntary candor: "Why, I did that. Or, no! What's she been doing?"

Ashley: "Really, Miss Garnett—"

Miss Garnett: "How can I tell you anything, if you don't tell me everything? You wouldn't wish me to betray confidence?"

Ashley: "No, certainly not. What was the confidence?"

Miss Garnett: "Well— But I shall have to know first what she's been doing. You must see that yourself, Mr. Ashley." He is silent. "Has she—has Isobel— been behaving—well, out of character?"

Ashley: "Very much indeed."

Miss Garnett: "I expected she would." She fetches a thoughtful sigh, and for her greater emotional convenience she sinks into an easy-chair and leans forward. "Oh dear! It is a scrape." Suddenly and imperatively: "Tell me exactly what she did, if you hope for any help whatever."

Ashley: "Why, she offered me a cocktail—"

Miss Garnett: "Oh, how good! I didn't suppose she would dare! Well?"

Ashley: "And she smoked cigarettes—"

Miss Garnett: "How perfectly divine! And what else?"

Ashley, coldly: "May I ask why you admire Miss Ramsey's behaving out of character so much? I think the smoking made her rather faint, and—"

Miss Garnett: "She would have let it kill her! Never tell me that girls have no moral courage!"

Ashley: "But what—what was the meaning of it all?"

Miss Garnett, thoughtfully: "I suppose if I got her in for it, I ought to get her out, even if I betray confidence."

Ashley: "It depends upon the confidence. What is it?"

Miss Garnett: "Why— But you're sure it's my duty?"

Ashley: "If you care what I think of her—"

Miss Garnett: "Oh, Mr. Ashley, you mustn't think it strange of Isobel, on my bended knees you mustn't! Why, don't you see? She was just doing it to disgust you!"

Ashley: "Disgust me?"

Miss Garnett: "Yes, and drive you back to Emily Fray."

Ashley: "Drive me ba—"

Miss Garnett: "If she thought you were engaged to Emily, when you were coming here all the time, and she wasn't quite sure that she hated to have you, don't you see it would be her duty to sacrifice herself, and— Oh, I suppose she's heard everything up there, and—" She catches herself up and runs out of the room, leaving Ashley to await the retarded descent of skirts which he hears on the stairs after the crash of the street door has announced Miss Garnett's escape. He stands with his back to the mantel, and faces Miss Ramsey as she enters the room.

VII

MISS RAMSEY, ASHLEY

Miss Ramsey, with the effect of cold surprise: "Mr. Ashley? I thought I heard — Wasn't Miss Garnett—"

Ashley: "She was. Did you think it was the street door closing on me?"

Miss Ramsey: "How should I know?" Then, courageously: "No, I didn't think it was. Why do you ask?" She moves uneasily about the room, with an air of studied inattention.

Ashley: "Because if you did, I can put you in the right, though I can't restore Miss Garnett's presence by my absence."

Miss Ramsey: "You're rather—enigmatical." A ring is heard; the maid pauses at the doorway. "I'm not at home, Nora." To Mr. Ashley: "It seems to be very close—"

Ashley: "It's my having been smoking."

Miss Ramsey: "Your having?" She goes to the window and tries to lift it.

Ashley: "Let me." He follows her to the window, where he stands beside her.

Miss Ramsey: "Now, she's seen me! And you here with me. Of course—"

Ashley: "I shouldn't mind. But I'm so sorry if—and I will go."

Miss Ramsey: "You can't go now—till she's round the corner. She'll keep looking back, and she'll think I made you."

Ashley: "But haven't you? Aren't you sending me back to Miss Fray to tell her that I must keep my engagement, though I care nothing for her, and care all the world for you? Isn't that what you want me to do?"

Miss Ramsey: "But you're not engaged to her! You just—"

Ashley: "Just what?"

Miss Ramsey, desperately: "You wish me to disgrace myself forever in your eyes. Well, I will; what does it matter now? I heard you telling Esther you were not engaged. I overheard you."

Ashley: "I fancied you must."

Miss Ramsey: "I tried to overhear! I eavesdropped! I wish you to know that."

Ashley: "And what do you wish me to do about it?"

Miss Ramsey: "I should think any self-respecting person would know. I'm not a self-respecting person." Her wandering gaze seems to fall for the first time upon the tray with the cocktails and glasses and cigarettes; she flies at the bell-button and presses it impetuously. As the maid appears: "Take these things away, Nora, please!" To Ashley when the maid has left the room: "Don't be afraid to say what you think of me!"

Ashley: "I think all the world of you. But I should merely like to ask—"

Miss Ramsey: "Oh, you can ask anything of me now!"

Ashley, with palpable insincerity: "I should like to ask why you don't respect yourself?"

Miss Ramsey: "Was that what you were going to ask? I know it wasn't. But I will tell you. Because I have been a fool."

Ashley: "Thank you. Now I will tell you what I was really going to ask. Why did you wish to drive me back to Miss Fray when you knew that I would be false to her a thousand times if I could only once be true to you?"

Miss Ramsey: "Now you are insulting me! And that is just the point. You may be a very clever lawyer, Mr. Ashley, and everybody says you are—very able, and talented, and all that, but you can't get round that point. You may torture any meaning you please out of my words, but I shall always say you brought it on yourself."

Ashley: "Brought what on?"

Miss Ramsey: "Mr. Ashley! I won't be cross-questioned."

Ashley: "Was that why you smoked, and poured cocktails out of an unopened bottle? Was it because you wished me to hate you, and remember my duty, and go back to Miss Fray? Well, it was a dead failure. It made me love you more than ever. I am a fool too, as you call it."

Miss Ramsey: "Say anything you please. I have given you the right. I shall not resent it. Go on."

Ashley: "I should only repeat myself. You must have known how much I care for you, Isobel. Do you mind my calling you Isobel?"

Miss Ramsey: "Not in the least if you wish to humiliate me by it. I should like you to trample on me in every way you can."

Ashley: "Trample on you? I would rather be run over by a steam-roller than tread on the least of your outlying feelings, dearest. Do you mind my saying dearest?"

Miss Ramsey: "I have told you that you can say anything you like. I deserve it. But oh, if you have a spark of pity—"

Ashley: "I'm a perfect conflagration of compassion, darling. Do you object to darling?"

Miss Ramsey, with starting tears: "It doesn't matter now." She has let her lovely length trail into the corner of the sofa, where she desperately reclines, supporting her elbow on the arm of it, and resting her drooping head on her hand. He draws a hassock up in front of her, and sits on it.

Ashley: "This represents kneeling at your feet. One doesn't do it literally any more, you know."

Miss Ramsey, in a hollow voice: "I should despise you if you did, and"—deeply murmurous—"I don't wish to despise you."

Ashley: "No, I understand that. You merely wish me to despise you. But why?"

Miss Ramsey, nervously: "You know."

Ashley: "But I don't know—Isobel, dearest, darling, if you will allow me to express myself so fully. How should I know?"

Miss Ramsey: "I've told you."

Ashley: "May I take your hand? For good-by!" He possesses himself of it. "It seems to go along with those expressions."

Miss Ramsey, self-contemptuously: "Oh yes."

Ashley: "Thank you. Where were we?"

Miss Ramsey, sitting up and recovering her hand: "You were saying good-by —"

Ashley: "Was I? But not before I had told you that I knew you were doing all that for my best good, and I wish—I wish you could have seen how exemplary you looked when you were trying to pour a cocktail out of a corked bottle, between your remarks on passionate fiction and puffs of the insidious cigarette! When the venomous tobacco began to get in its deadly work, and you turned pale and reeled a little, and called for air, it made me mentally vow to go back to Miss Fray instantly, whether I was engaged to her or not, and cut out poor old Brooks—"

Miss Ramsey: "Was it Mr. Brooks? I didn't hear the name exactly."

Ashley: "When I was telling Miss Garnett? I ought to have spoken louder, but I wasn't sure at the time you were listening. Though as you were saying, what does it matter now?"

Miss Ramsey: "Did I say that?"

Ashley: "Words to that effect. And they have made me feel how unworthy of you I am. I'm not heroic—by nature. But I could be, if you made me—by art —"

Miss Ramsey, springing to her feet indignantly: "Now, you are ridiculing me —you are making fun of me."

Ashley, gathering himself up from his hassock with difficulty, and confronting her: "Do I look like a man who would dare to make fun of you? I am half a head shorter than you, and in moral grandeur you overtop me so that I would always have to wear a high hat when I was with you."

Miss Ramsey, thoughtfully: "Plenty of girls are that way, now. But if you are ashamed of my being tall—" Flashingly, and with starting tears.

Ashley: "Ashamed! I can always look up to you, you can always stoop to me!" He stretches his arms toward her.

Miss Ramsey, recoiling bewildered: "Wait! We haven't got to that yet."

Ashley: "Oh, Isobel—dearest—darling! We've got past it! We're on the home stretch, now."

<h1 style="text-align:center">XIX</h1>

THE NIGHT BEFORE CHRISTMAS
A MORALITY
I
MR. AND MRS. CLARENCE FOUNTAIN

Mrs. Clarence Fountain, backing into the room, and closing the door noiselessly before looking round: "Oh, you poor thing! I can see that you are dead, at the first glance. I'm dead myself, for that matter." She is speaking to her husband, who clings with one hand to the chimney-piece, and supports his back with the other; from this hand a little girl's long stocking lumpily dangles; Mrs. Fountain, turning round, observes it. "Not finished yet? But I don't wonder! I wonder you've even begun. Well, now, I will take hold with you." In token of the aid she is going to give, Mrs. Fountain sinks into a chair and rolls a distracted eye over the littered and tumbled room. "It's worse than I thought it would be. You ought to have smoothed the papers out and laid them in a pile as fast as you unwrapped the things; that is the way I always do; and wound the strings up and put them one side. Then you wouldn't have had to wade round in them. I suppose I oughtn't to have left it to you, but if I had let you put the children to bed you know you'd have told them stories and kept them all night over their prayers. And as it was each of them wanted to put in a special Christmas clause; I know what kind of Christmas clause I should have put in if I'd been frank! I'm not sure it's right to keep up the deception. One comfort, the oldest ones don't believe in it any more than we do. Dear! I did think at one time this afternoon I should have to be brought home in an ambulance; it would have been a convenience, with all the packages. I simply marvel at their delivery wagons getting them here."

Fountain, coming to the table, where she sits, and taking up one of the toys with which it is strewn: "They haven't all of them."

Mrs. Fountain: "What do you mean by all of them?"

Fountain: "I mean half." He takes up a mechanical locomotive and stuffs it into the stocking he holds.

Mrs. Fountain, staying his hand: "What are you doing? Putting Jimmy's engine into Susy's stocking! She'll be perfectly insulted when she finds it, for she'll know you weren't paying the least attention, and you can't blame Santa Claus for it with her. If that's what you've been doing with the other stockings— But there aren't any others. Don't tell me you've just begun! Well, I could simply cry."

Fountain, dropping into the chair on the other side of the table, under the shelter of a tall Christmas tree standing on it: "Do you call unwrapping a whole car-load of truck and getting it sorted, just beginning? I've been slaving here from the dawn of time, and I had to have some leisure for the ghosts of my own Christmases when I was little. I didn't have to wade round in the wrappings of my presents in those days. But it isn't the sad memories that take it out of you; it's the happy ones. I've never had a ghastlier half-hour than I've just spent in the humiliating multiplicity of these gifts. All the old birthdays and wedding-days and Fourth of Julys and home-comings and children's christenings I've ever had came trooping back. There oughtn't to be any gay anniversaries; they should be forbidden by law. If I could only have recalled a few dangerous fevers and funerals!"

Mrs. Fountain: "Clarence! Don't say such a thing; you'll be punished for it. I know how you suffer from those gloomy feelings, and I pity you. You ought to bear up against them. If I gave way! You must think about something cheerful in the future when the happiness of the past afflicts you, and set one against the other; life isn't all a vale of tears. You must keep your mind fixed on the work before you. I don't believe it's the number of the packages here that's broken you down. It's the shopping that's worn you out; I'm sure I'm a mere thread. And I had been at it from immediately after breakfast; and I lunched in one of the stores with ten thousand suburbans who had come pouring in with the first of their unnatural trains: I did hope I should have some of the places to myself; but they were every one jammed. And you came up from your office about four, perfectly fresh."

Fountain: "Fresh! Yes, quite dewy from a day's fight with the beasts at Ephesus on the eve of Christmas week."

Mrs. Fountain: "Well, don't be cynical, Clarence, on this, of all nights of the year. You know how sorry I always am for what you have to go through down there, and I suppose it's worse, as you say, at this season than any other time of year. It's the terrible concentration of everything just before Christmas that makes it so killing. I really don't know which of the places was the worst; the big department stores or the separate places for jewelry and toys and books and stationery and antiques; they were all alike, and all maddening. And the rain outside, and everybody coming in reeking; though I don't believe that sunshine would have been any better; there'd have been more of them. I declare, it made my heart ache for those poor creatures behind the counters, and I don't know whether I suffered most for them when they kept up a ghastly cheerfulness in their attention or were simply insulting in their indifference. I know they must be all dead by this time. 'Going up?' 'Going down?' 'Ca-ish!' 'Here, boy!' I believe it will ring in my ears as long as I live. And the whiz of those overhead wire things, and having to wait ages for your change, and then drag your tatters out of the stores into the streets! If I hadn't had you with me at the last I should certainly have dropped."

Fountain: "Yes, and what had become of your good resolutions about doing all your Christmas shopping in July?"

Mrs. Fountain: "My good resolutions? Really, Clarence, sometimes if it were not cruelty to animals I should like to hit you. My good— You know that you suggested that plan, and it wasn't even original with you. The papers have been talking about it for years; but when you brought it up as such a new idea, I fell in with it to please you—"

Fountain: "Now, look out, Lucy!"

Mrs. Fountain: "Yes, to please you, and to help you forget the Christmas worry, just as I've been doing to-night. You never spare me."

Fountain: "Stick to the record. Why didn't you do your Christmas shopping in July?"

Mrs. Fountain: "Why didn't I? Did you expect me to do my Christmas shopping down at Sculpin Beach, where I spent the whole time from the middle of June till the middle of September? Why didn't you do the Christmas shopping in July? You had the stores under your nose here from the beginning till the end of summer, with nothing in the world to hinder you, and not a chick or a child to look after."

Fountain: "Oh, I like that. You think I was leading a life of complete leisure here, with the thermometer among the nineties nine-tenths of the time?"

Mrs. Fountain: "I only know you were bragging in all your letters about your bath and your club, and the folly of any one going away from the cool, comfortable town in the summer. I suppose you'll say that was to keep me from feeling badly at leaving you. When it was only for the children's sake! I will let you take them the next time."

Fountain: "While you look after my office? And you think the stores are full of Christmas things in July, I suppose."

Mrs. Fountain: "I never thought so; and now I hope you see the folly of that idea. No, Clarence. We must be logical in everything. You can't get rid of Christmas shopping at Christmas-time."

Fountain, shouting wrathfully: "Then I say get rid of Christmas!"

II
MR. FRANK WATKINS, MRS. FOUNTAIN, FOUNTAIN

Watkins, opening the door for himself and struggling into the room with an armful of parcels: "I'm with you there, Clarence. Christmas is at the root of Christmas shopping, and Christmas giving, and all the rest of it. Oh, you needn't be afraid, Lucy. I didn't hear any epithets; just caught the drift of your argument through the keyhole. I've been kicking at the door ever since you began. Where shall I dump these things?"

Mrs. Fountain: "Oh, you poor boy! Here—anywhere—on the floor—on the sofa—on the table." She clears several spaces and helps Watkins unload. "Clarence! I'm surprised at you. What are you thinking of?"

Fountain: "I'm thinking that if this goes on, I'll let somebody else arrange the presents."

Watkins: "If I saw a man coming into my house with a load like this to-night, I'd throw him into the street. But living in a ninth-story flat like you, it might hurt him."

Mrs. Fountain, reading the inscriptions on the packages: "'For Benny from his uncle Frank.' Oh, how sweet of you, Frank! And here's a kiss for his uncle Frank." She embraces him with as little interruption as possible. "'From Uncle Frank to Jim.' Oh, I know what that is!" She feels the package over. "And this is for 'Susy from her aunt Sue.' Oh, I knew she would remember her namesake. 'For Maggie. Merry Christmas from Mrs. Watkins.' 'Bridget, with Mrs. Watkins's best wishes for a Merry Christmas.' Both the girls! But it's like Sue; she never forgets anybody. And what's this for Clarence? I must know! Not a bath-gown?" Undoing it: "I simply must see it. Blue! His very color!" Holding it up: "From you, Frank?" He nods. "Clarence!"

Watkins: "If Fountain tries to kiss me, I'll—"

Fountain: "I wouldn't kiss you for a dozen bath-gowns." Lifting it up from the floor where Mrs. Fountain has dropped it: "It is rather nice."

Watkins: "Don't overwhelm me."

Mrs. Fountain, dancing about with a long, soft roll in her hand: "Oh, oh, oh! She saw me gloating on it at Shumaker's! I do wonder if it is."

Fountain, reaching for it: "Why, open it—"

Mrs. Fountain: "You dare! No, it shall be opened the very last thing in the morning, now, to punish you! How is poor Sue? I saw her literally dropping by the way at Shumaker's."

Watkins, making for the door: "Well, she must have got up again. I left her registering a vow that if ever she lived to see another Christmas she would leave the country months before the shopping began. She called down maledictions on all the recipients of her gifts and wished them the worst harm that can befall the wicked."

Mrs. Fountain: "Poor Sue! She simply lives to do people good, and I can understand exactly how she feels toward them. I'll be round bright and early to-morrow to thank her. Why do you go?"

Watkins: "Well, I can't stay here all night, and I'd better let you and Clarence finish up." He escapes from her detaining embrace and runs out.

III
MRS. FOUNTAIN, FOUNTAIN

Mrs. Fountain, intent upon her roll: "How funny he is! I wonder if he did hear anything but our scolding voices? Where were we?"

Fountain: "I had just called you a serpent."

Mrs. Fountain, with amusement: "No, really?" Feeling the parcel: "If it's that Spanish lace scarf I can tell her it was machine lace. I saw it at the first glance. But poor Sue has no taste. I suppose I must stand it. But I can't bear to think what she's given the girls and children. She means well. Did you really say serpent, Clarence? You never called me just that before."

Fountain: "No, but you called me a laughing hyena, and said I scoffed at everything sacred."

Mrs. Fountain: "I can't remember using the word hyena, exactly, though I do think the way you talk about Christmas is dreadful. But I take back the laughing hyena."

Fountain: "And I take back the serpent. I meant dove, anyway. But it's this Christmas-time when a man gets so tired he doesn't know what he's saying."

Mrs. Fountain: "Well, you're good, anyway, dearest, whatever you say; and now I'm going to help you arrange the things. I suppose there'll be lots more to-morrow, but we must get rid of these now. Don't you wish nobody would do anything for us? Just the children—dear little souls! I don't believe but what we can make Jim and Susy believe in Santa Claus again; Benny is firm in the faith; he put him into his prayer. I declare, his sweetness almost broke my heart." At a knock: "Who's that, I wonder? Come in! Oh, it's you, Maggie. Well?"

IV
THE FOUNTAINS, FOUNTAIN'S SISTERS

Maggie: "It's Mr. Fountain's sisters just telephoned up."

Mrs. Fountain: "Have them come up at once, Maggie, of course." As Maggie goes out: "Another interruption! If it's going to keep on like this! Shouldn't you have thought they might have sent their presents?"

Fountain: "I thought something like it in Frank's case; but I didn't say it."

Mrs. Fountain: "And I don't know why I say it, now. It's because I'm so tired I don't know what I am saying. Do forgive me! It's this terrible Christmas spirit that gets into me. But now you'll see how nice I can be to them." At a tap on the door: "Come in! Come in! Don't mind our being in all this mess. So darling of you to come! You can help cheer Clarence up; you know his Christmas Eve dumps." She runs to them and clasps them in her arms with several half-open packages dangling from her hands and contrasting their disarray with the neatness of their silk-ribboned and tissue-papered parcels which their embrace makes meet at her back. "Minnie! Aggie! To lug here, when you ought to be at home in bed dying of fatigue! But it's just like you, both of you. Did you ever see anything like the stores to-day? Do sit down, or swoon on the floor, or anything. Let me have those wretched bundles which are simply killing you." She looks at the different packages. "'For Benny from Grandpa.' 'For a good girl, from Susy's grandmother.' 'Jim, from Aunt Minnie and Aunt Aggie.' 'Lucy, with love from Aggie and Minnie.' And Clarence! What hearts you have got! Well, I always say there never were such thoughtful girls, and you always show such taste and such originality. I long to get at the things." She keeps fingering the large bundle marked with her husband's name. "Not—not—a—"

Minnie: "Yes, a bath-robe. Unless you give him a cigar-case it's about the only thing you can give a man."

Aggie: "Minnie thought of it and I chose it. Blue, because it's his color. Try it on, Clarence, and if it's too long—"

Mrs. Fountain: "Yes, do, dear! Let's see you with it on." While the girls are fussily opening the robe, she manages to push her brother's gift behind the door. Then, without looking round at her husband. "It isn't a bit too long. Just the very—" Looking: "Well, it can easily be taken up at the hem. I can do it to-morrow." She abandons him to his awkward isolation while she chatters on with his sisters. "Sit down; I insist! Don't think of going. Did you see that frightful pack of people when the cab horse fell down in front of Shumaker's?"

Minnie: "See it?"

Aggie: "We were in the midst of it! I wonder we ever got out alive. It's enough to make you wish never to see another Christmas as long as you live."

Minnie: "A great many won't live. There will be more grippe, and more pneumonia, and more appendicitis from those jams of people in the stores!"

Aggie: "The germs must have been swarming."

Fountain: "Lucy was black with them when we got home."

Mrs. Fountain: "Don't pay the slightest attention to him, girls. He'll probably be the first to sneeze himself."

Minnie: "I don't know about sneezing. I shall only be too glad if I don't have nervous prostration from it."

Aggie: "I'm glad we got our motor-car just in time. Any one that goes in the trolleys now will take their life in their hand." The girls rise and move toward the door. "Well, we must go on now. We're making a regular round; you can't trust the delivery wagons at a time like this. Good-by. Merry Christmas to the children. They're fast asleep by this time, I suppose."

Minnie: "I only wish I was!"

Mrs. Fountain: "I believe you, Minnie. Good-by. Good night. Good night, Aggie. Clarence, go to the elevator with them! Or no, he can't in that ridiculous bath-gown!" Turning to Fountain as the door closes: "Now I've done it."

V
MRS. FOUNTAIN, FOUNTAIN

Fountain: "It isn't a thing you could have wished to phrase that way, exactly."

Mrs. Fountain: "And you made me do it. Never thanking them, or anything, and standing there like I don't know what, and leaving the talk all to me. And now, making me lose my temper again, when I wanted to be so nice to you. Well, it is no use trying, and from this on I won't. Clarence!" She has opened the parcel addressed to herself and now stands transfixed with joy and wonder. "See what the girls have given me! The very necklace I've been longing for at Planets', and denying myself for the last fortnight! Well, never will I say your sisters are mean again."

Fountain: "You ought to have said that to them."

Mrs. Fountain: "It quite reconciles one to Christmas. What? Oh, that was rather nasty. You know I didn't mean it. I was so excited I didn't know what I was saying. I'm sure nobody ever got on better with sisters-in-law, and that shows my tact; if I do make a slip, now and then, I can always get out of it. They will understand. Do you think it was very nice of them to flaunt their new motor in my face? But of course anything your family does is perfect, and always was, though I must say this necklace is sweet of them. I wonder they had the taste." A tap on the door is heard. "Come in, Maggie!" Sotto voce. "Take it off." She snatches his bath-robe and tosses it behind the door.

VI
WILBUR HAZARD, THE FOUNTAINS

Hazard: "I suppose I can come in, even if I'm not Maggie. Catch, Fountain." He tosses a large bundle to Fountain. "It's huge, but it isn't hefty." He turns to go out again.

Mrs. Fountain: "Oh, oh, oh! Don't go! Come in and help us. What have you brought Clarence! May I feel?"

Hazard: "You can look, if you like. I'm rather proud of it. There's only one other thing you can give a man, and I said, 'No, not a cigar-case. Fountain smokes enough already, but if a bath-robe can induce him to wash—'" He goes out.

Mrs. Fountain, screaming after him through the open door: "Oh, how good! Come back and see it on him." She throws the bath-robe over Fountain's shoulders.

Hazard, looking in again: "Perfect fit, just as the Jew said, and the very color for Fountain." He vanishes, shutting the door behind him.

VII

MRS. FOUNTAIN, FOUNTAIN

Mrs. Fountain: "How coarse! Well, my dear, I don't know where you picked up your bachelor friends. I hope this is the last of them."

Fountain: "Hazard's the only one who has survived your rigorous treatment. But he always had a passion for cold shoulder, poor fellow. As bath-robes go, this isn't bad." He gets his arms into it, and walks up and down. "Heigh?"

Mrs. Fountain: "Yes, it is pretty good. But the worst of Christmas is that it rouses up all your old friends."

Fountain: "They feel so abnormally good, confound them. I suppose poor old Hazard half killed himself looking this thing up and building the joke to go with it."

Mrs. Fountain: "Well, take it off, now, and come help me with the children's presents. You're quite forgetting about them, and it'll be morning and you'll have the little wretches swarming in before you can turn round. Dear little souls! I can sympathize with their impatience, of course. But what are you going to do with these bath-robes? You can't wear four bath-robes."

Fountain: "I can change them every day. But there ought to be seven. This hood is rather a new wrinkle, though, isn't it? I suppose it's for a voyage, and you pull it up over your head when you come through the corridor back to your stateroom. We shall have to go to Europe, Lucy."

Mrs. Fountain: "I would go to Asia, Africa, and Oceanica, to escape another Christmas. Now if there are any more bath-robes— Come in, Maggie."

VIII

MAGGIE, THE FOUNTAINS

Maggie, bringing in a bundle: "Something a District Messenger brought. Will you sign for it, ma'am?"

Mrs. Fountain: "You sign, Clarence. If I know anything about the look and the feel of a bundle, this is another bath-robe, but I shall soon see." While she is cutting the string and tearing the wrappings away, Fountain signs and Maggie goes. Mrs. Fountain shakes out the folds of the robe. "Well, upon my word, I should think there was conspiracy to insult you, Clarence. I should like to know who has had the effrontery— What's on it?"

Fountain, reading from the card which had fallen out of the garment to the floor: "'With Christmas greetings from Mrs. Arthur J. Gibby.'"

Mrs. Fountain, dropping the robe and seizing the card: "Mrs. Arthur J. Gibby! Well, upon my word, this is impudence. It's not only impudence, it's indelicacy. And I had always thought she was the very embodiment of refinement, and I've gone about saying so. Now I shall have to take it back. The idea of a lady sending a bath-robe to a gentleman! What next, I wonder! What right has Mrs. Gibby to send you a bath-robe? Don't prevaricate! Remember that the truth is the only thing that can save you. Matters must have gone pretty far, when a woman could send you anything so—intimate. What are you staring at with that paper? You needn't hope to divert my mind by—"

Fountain, giving her the paper in which the robe came: "Seems to be for Mrs. Clarence Fountain."

Mrs. Fountain, snatching it from him: "What! It is, it is! Oh, poor dear Lilly! How can you ever forgive me? She saw me looking at it to-day at Shumaker's, and it must have come into her head in despair what else to get me. But it was a perfect inspiration—for it was just what I was longing for. Why"—laughing hysterically while she holds up the robe, and turns it this way and that—"I might have seen at a glance that it wasn't a man's, with this lace on and this silk hood, and"—she hurries into it, and pulls it forward, looking down at either side—"it's just the right length, and if it was made for me it couldn't fit me better. What a joke I shall have with Lilly, when I tell her about it. I sha'n't spare myself a bit!"

Fountain: "Then I hope you'll spare me. I have some little delicacy of feeling, and I don't like the notion of a lady's giving me a bath-robe. It's—intimate. I don't know where you picked up your girl friends."

Mrs. Fountain, capering about joyfully: "Oh, how funny you are, darling! But go on. I don't mind it, now. And you may be glad you've got off so easily. Only now if there are any more bath-robes—" A timid rap is heard at the door.

"Come in, Maggie!" The door is slowly set ajar, then flung suddenly wide open, and Jim and Susy in their night-gowns rush dancing and exulting in.

IX
JIM, SUSY, THE FOUNTAINS

Susy: "We've caught you, we've caught you."

Jim: "I just bet it was you, and now I've won, haven't I, mother?"

Susy: "And I've won, too, haven't I, father?" Arrested at sight of her father in the hooded bath-gown: "He does look like Santa Claus, doesn't he, Jimmy? But the real Santa Claus would be all over snow, and a long, white beard. You can't fool us!"

Jim: "You can't fool us! We know you, we know you! And mother dressed up, too! There isn't any Mrs. Santa Claus, and that proves it!"

Mrs. Fountain, severely: "Dreadful little things! Who said you might come here? Go straight back to bed, this minute, or— Will you send them back, Clarence, and not stand staring so? What are you thinking of?"

Fountain, dreamily: "Nothing. Merely wondering what we shall do when we've got rid of our superstitions. Shall we be the better for it, or even the wiser?"

Mrs. Fountain: "What put that question into your head? Christmas, I suppose; and that's another reason for wishing there was no such thing. If I had my way, there wouldn't be."

Jim: "Oh, mother!"

Susy: "No Christmas?"

Mrs. Fountain: "Well, not for disobedient children who get out of bed and come in, spoiling everything. If you don't go straight back, it will be the last time, Santa Claus or no Santa Claus."

Jim: "And if we go right back?"

Susy: "And promise not to come in any more?"

Mrs. Fountain: "Well, we'll see how you keep your promise. If you don't, that's the end of Christmas in this house."

Jim: "It's a bargain, then! Come on, Susy!"

Susy: "And we do it for you, mother. And for you, father. We just came in for fun, anyway."

Jim: "We just came for a surprise."

Mrs. Fountain, kissing them both: "Well, then, if it was only for fun, we'll excuse you this time. Run along, now, that's good children. Clarence!"

X

MRS. FOUNTAIN, FOUNTAIN

Fountain: "Well?" He looks up at her from where he has dropped into a chair beside the table strewn with opened and unopened gifts at the foot of the Christmas tree.

Mrs. Fountain: "What are you mooning about?"

Fountain: "What if it was all a fake? Those thousands and hundreds of thousands of churches that pierce the clouds with their spires; those millions of ministers and missionaries; those billions of worshipers, sitting and standing and kneeling, and singing and praying; those nuns and monks, and brotherhoods and sisterhoods, with their ideals of self-denial, and their duties to the sick and poor; those martyrs that died for the one true faith, and those other martyrs of the other true faiths whom the one true faith tortured and killed; those masses and sermons and ceremonies, what if they were all a delusion, a mistake, a misunderstanding? What if it were all as unlike the real thing, if there is any real thing, as this pagan Christmas of ours is as unlike a Christian Christmas?"

Mrs. Fountain, springing up: "I knew it! I knew that it was this Christmas giving that was making you morbid again. Can't you shake it off and be cheerful—like me? I'm sure I have to bear twice as much of it as you have. I've been shopping the whole week, and you've been just this one afternoon." She begins to catch her breath, and fails in searching for her handkerchief in the folds of her dress under the bath-robe.

Fountain, offering his handkerchief: "Take mine."

Mrs. Fountain, catching it from him, and hiding her face in it on the table: "You ought to help me bear up, and instead of that you fling yourself on my sympathies and break me down." Lifting her face: "And if it was all a fake, as you say, and an illusion, what would you do, what would you give people in place of it?"

Fountain: "I don't know."

Mrs. Fountain: "What would you have in place of Christmas itself?"

Fountain: "I don't know."

Mrs. Fountain: "Well, then, I wouldn't set myself up to preach down everything—in a blue bath-gown. You've no idea how ridiculous you are."

Fountain: "Oh, yes, I have. I can see you. You look like one of those blue nuns in Rome. But I don't remember any lace on them."

Mrs. Fountain: "Well, you don't look like a blue monk, you needn't flatter yourself, for there are none. You look like— What are you thinking about?"

Fountain: "Oh, nothing. What do you suppose is in all these packages here? Useful things, that we need, that we must have? You know without looking that it's the superfluity of naughtiness in one form or other. And the givers of these gifts, they had to give them, just as we've had to give dozens of gifts ourselves. We ought to have put on our cards, 'With the season's bitterest grudges,' 'In hopes of a return,' 'With a hopeless sense of the folly,' 'To pay a hateful debt,' 'With impotent rage and despair.'"

Mrs. Fountain: "I don't deny it, Clarence. You're perfectly right; I almost wish we had put it. How it would have made them hop! But they'd have known it was just the way they felt themselves."

Fountain, going on thoughtfully: "It's the cap-sheaf of the social barbarism we live in, the hideous hypocrisy. It's no use to put it on religion. The Jews keep Christmas, too, and we know what they think of Christianity as a belief. No, we've got to go further back, to the Pagan Saturnalia— Well, I renounce the whole affair, here and now. I'm going to spend the rest of the night bundling these things up, and to-morrow I'm going to spend the day in a taxi, going round and giving them back to the fools that sent them."

Mrs. Fountain: "And I'm going with you. I hate it as much as you do— Come in, Maggie!"

XI

MAGGIE, MRS. FOUNTAIN, FOUNTAIN

Maggie: "Something the elevator-boy says he forgot. It came along with the last one."

Mrs. Fountain, taking a bundle from her: "If this is another bath-robe, Clarence! It is, as I live. Now if it is a woman sending it—" She picks up a card which falls out of the robe as she unfolds it. "'Love the Giver,' indeed! Now, Clarence, I insist, I demand—"

Fountain: "Hold on, hold on, my dear. The last bath-robe that came from a woman was for you."

Mrs. Fountain: "So it was. I don't know what I was thinking about; and I do beg your par— But this is a man's bath-robe!"

Fountain, taking the card which she mechanically stretches out to him: "And a man sends it—old Fellows. Can't you read print? Ambrose J. Fellows, and a message in writing: 'It was a toss-up between this and a cigar-case, and the bath-robe won. Hope you haven't got any other thoughtful friends.'"

Mrs. Fountain: "Oh, very brilliant, giving me a start like this! I shall let Mr. Fellows know— What is it, Maggie? Open the door, please."

Maggie, opening: "It's just a District Messenger."

Fountain, ironically: "Oh, only a District Messenger." He signs the messenger's slip, while his wife receives from Maggie a bundle which she regards with suspicion.

XII

MRS. FOUNTAIN, FOUNTAIN

Mrs. Fountain: "'From Uncle Philip for Clarence.' Well, Uncle Philip, if you have sent Clarence— Clarence!" breaking into a whimper: "It is, it is! It's another."

Fountain: "Well, that only makes the seventh, and just enough for every day in the week. It's quite my ideal. Now, if there's nothing about a cigar-case— Hello!" He feels in the pocket of the robe and brings out a cigar-case, from which a slip of paper falls: "'Couldn't make up my mind between them, so send both. Uncle Phil.' Well, this is the last stroke of Christmas insanity."

Mrs. Fountain: "His brain simply reeled under it, and gave way. It shows what Christmas really comes to with a man of strong intellect like Uncle Phil."

Fountain, opening the case: "Oh, I don't know! He's put some cigars in here— in a lucid interval, probably. There's hope yet."

Mrs. Fountain, in despair: "No, Clarence, there's no hope. Don't flatter yourself. The only way is to bundle back all their presents and never, never, never give or receive another one. Come! Let's begin tying them up at once; it will take us the rest of the night." A knock at the door. "Come, Maggie."

XIII

JIM AND SUSY, MRS. FOUNTAIN, FOUNTAIN

Jim and Susy, pushing in: "We can't sleep, mother. May we have a pillow fight to keep us amused till we're drowsy?"

Mrs. Fountain, desolately: "Yes, go and have your pillow fight. It doesn't matter now. We're sending the presents all back, anyway." She begins frantically wrapping some of the things up.

Susy: "Oh, father, are you sending them back?"

Jim: "She's just making believe. Isn't she, father?"

Fountain: "Well, I'm not so sure of that. If she doesn't do it, I will."

Mrs. Fountain, desisting: "Will you go right back to bed?"

Jim and Susy: "Yes, we will."

Mrs. Fountain: "And to sleep, instantly?"

Jim and Susy, in succession: "We won't keep awake a minute longer."

Mrs. Fountain: "Very well, then, we'll see. Now be off with you." As they put their heads together and go out laughing: "And remember, if you come here another single time, back go every one of the presents."

Fountain: "As soon as ever Santa Claus can find a moment for it."

Jim, derisively: "Oh, yes, Santa Claus!"

Susy: "I guess if you wait for Santa Claus to take them back!"

XIV

MRS. FOUNTAIN, FOUNTAIN

Mrs. Fountain: "Tiresome little wretches. Of course we can't expect them to keep up the self-deception."

Fountain: "They'll grow to another. When they're men and women they'll pretend that Christmas is delightful, and go round giving people the presents that they've worn their lives out in buying and getting together. And they'll work themselves up into the notion that they are really enjoying it, when they know at the bottom of their souls that they loathe the whole job."

Mrs. Fountain: "There you are with your pessimism again! And I had just begun to feel cheerful about it!"

Fountain: "Since when? Since I proposed sending this rubbish back to the givers with our curse?"

Mrs. Fountain: "No, I was thinking what fun it would be if we could get up a sort of Christmas game, and do it just among relations and intimate friends."

Fountain: "Ah, I wish you luck of it. Then the thing would begin to have some reality, and just as in proportion as people had the worst feelings in giving the presents, their best feeling would be hurt in getting them back."

Mrs. Fountain: "Then why did you ever think of it?"

Fountain: "To keep from going mad. Come, let's go on with this job of sorting the presents, and putting them in the stockings and hanging them up on the tree and laying them round the trunk of it. One thing: it's for the last time. As soon as Christmas week is over, I shall inaugurate an educational campaign against the whole Christmas superstition. It must be extirpated root and branch, and the extirpation must begin in the minds of the children; we old fools are hopeless; we must die in it; but the children can be saved. We must organize and make a house-to-house fight; and I'll begin in our own house. To-morrow, as soon as the children have made themselves thoroughly sick with candy and cake and midday dinner, I will appeal to their reason, and get them to agree to drop it; to sign the Anti-Christmas pledge; to—"

Mrs. Fountain: "Clarence! I have an idea."

Fountain: "Not a bright one?"

Mrs. Fountain: "Yes, a bright one, even if you didn't originate it. Have Christmas confined entirely to children—to the very youngest—to children that believe firmly in Santa Claus."

Fountain: "Oh, hello! Wouldn't that leave Jim and Susy out? I couldn't have them left out."

Mrs. Fountain: "That's true. I didn't think of that. Well, say, to children that either believe or pretend to believe in him. What's that?" She stops at a faint, soft sound on the door. "It's Maggie with her hands so full she's pushing with her elbow. Come in, Maggie, come in. Come in! Don't you hear me? Come in, I say! Oh, it isn't Maggie, of course! It's those worthless, worthless little wretches, again." She runs to the door calling out, "Naughty, naughty,

naughty!" as she runs. Then, flinging the door wide, with a final cry of "Naughty, I say!" she discovers a small figure on the threshold, nightgowned to its feet, and looking up with a frightened, wistful face. "Why, Benny!" She stoops down and catches the child in her arms, and presses him tight to her neck, and bends over, covering his head with kisses. "What in the world are you doing here, you poor little lamb? Is mother's darling walking in his sleep? What did you want, my pet? Tell mudda, do! Whisper it in mudda's big ear! Can't you tell mudda? What? Whisper a little louder, love! We're not angry with you, sweetness. Now, try to speak louder. Is that Santa Claus? No, dearest, that's just dadda. Santa Claus hasn't come yet, but he will soon. What? Say it again. Is there any Santa Claus? Why, who else could have brought all these presents? Presents for Benny and Jim and Susy and mudda, and seven bath-gowns for dadda. Isn't that funny? Seven! And one for mudda. What? I can't quite hear you, pet. Are we going to send the presents back? Why, who ever heard of such a thing? Jim said so? And Susy? Well, I will settle with them, when I come to them. You don't want me to? Well, I won't, then, if Benny doesn't want mudda to. I'll just give them a kiss apiece, pop in their big ears. What? You've got something for Santa Claus to give them? What? Where? In your crib? And shall we go and get it? For mudda too? And dadda? Oh, my little angel!" She begins to cry over him, and to kiss him again. "You'll break my heart with your loveliness. He wants to kiss you too, dadda." She puts the boy into his father's arms; then catches him back and runs from the room with him. Fountain resumes the work of filling the long stocking he had begun with; then he takes up a very short sock. He has that in his hand when Mrs. Fountain comes back, wiping her eyes. "He'll go to sleep now, I guess; he was half dreaming when he came in here. I should think, when you saw how Benny believed in it, you'd be ashamed of saying a word against Christmas."

Fountain: "Who's said anything against it? I've just been arguing for it, and trying to convince you that for the sake of little children like Benny it ought to be perpetuated to the end of the world. It began with the childhood of the race, in the rejuvenescence of the spirit."

Mrs. Fountain: "Didn't you say that Christmas began with the pagans? How monstrously you prevaricate!"

Fountain: "That was merely a figure of speech. And besides, since you've been out with Benny, I've been thinking, and I take back everything I've said or thought against Christmas; I didn't really think it. I've been going back in my mind to that first Christmas we had together, and it's cheered me up wonderfully."

Mrs. Fountain, tenderly: "Have you, dearest? I always think of it. If you could have seen Benny, how I left him, just now?"

Fountain: "I shouldn't mind seeing him, and I shouldn't care if I gave a glance at poor old Jim and Susy. I'd like to reassure them about not sending back the presents." He puts his arm round her and presses her toward the door.

Mrs. Fountain: "How sweet you are! And how funny! And good!" She accentuates each sentiment with a kiss. "And don't you suppose I felt sorry for you, making you go round with me the whole afternoon, and then leaving you to take the brunt of arranging the presents? Now I'll tell you: next year, I will do my Christmas shopping in July. It's the only way."

Fountain: "No, there's a better way. As you were saying, they don't have the Christmas things out. The only way is to do our Christmas shopping the day after Christmas; everything will be round still, and dog-cheap. Come, we'll begin day after to-morrow."

Mrs. Fountain: "We will, we will!"

Fountain: "Do you think we will?"

Mrs. Fountain: "Well, we'll say we will." They laugh together, and then he kisses her.

Fountain: "Even if it goes on in the same old way, as long as we have each other—"

Mrs. Fountain: "And the children."

Fountain: "I forgot the children!"

Mrs. Fountain: "Oh, how delightful you are!"

9 781835 915509